CU00994064

Let Slip the Dogs of War

Let Slip the Dogs of War

RICHARD GRAYSON

ROBERT HALE · LONDON

ISBN 0 7090 7090 X

Robert Hale Limited
Clerkenwell House
Clerkenwell Green
London EC1R 0HT

2 4 6 8 10 9 7 5 3 1

Typeset in 11/16 pt Sabon
by Derek Doyle & Associates, Liverpool.
Printed in Great Britain by
St Edmundsbury Press, Bury St Edmunds, Suffolk.
Bound by Woolnough Bookbinding Limited.

'Cry, "Havoc!" and let slip the dogs of war.'

Shakespeare – *Julius Caesar*

1

That evening there were relatively few travellers passing through the Gare de Montparnasse and for the most part they were leaving Paris, heading for their homes at the end of the day's work. So Gautier found a fiacre without difficulty. He was not an impatient man, but for once he had reasons for wishing to hurry. For the past two days he had been attending a meeting of European police chiefs that had been held in a 17th-century château just outside Paris. In the normal way the Sûreté would have been represented at the meeting by Gustave Courtrand, its Director General, but Courtrand was indisposed and had deputed Gautier to take his place. Gautier had not enjoyed the meeting nor had he expected to.

In his experience meetings of that type, the ostensible purpose of which was to allow an exchange of information on police methods, achieved very little. Those who attended came ready to talk, but reluctant to listen. They were eager to present their country's achievements in policing and crime prevention in as favourable a light as possible and, in Europe at least, though the names of police institutions varied, their methods of working were very similar. As a result the meetings often consisted of no more than a series of lectures, usually vainglorious and tiresomely similar, most of which had to be translated, sentence by sentence by interpreters. There were few opportunities for questions, but many for compliments and for grateful tributes to the hosts, in this case the French, for their hospitality which, in Gautier's view, was typically excessive.

So after the meeting had finally ended, Gautier had been glad to hurry back to Paris and the prospect of an evening with his mistress Ingrid Van de Velde. He supposed one might describe Ingrid as his mistress, even though their relationship was not one of which most Frenchmen would approve. She was Dutch, fair-haired and attractive, clever, once married but now divorced, a journalist who had been successful in what was a man's world. Because of her success she was busy and since they had met a few months ago, their opportunities for making love had been limited to less than a dozen nights. But what they had lacked in frequency had been more than requited in passion, which was why after two days of boring, masculine company, he was looking forward to the intimate supper in her apartment which she had promised him. He also had a feeling that the lovemaking they enjoyed was gradually being strengthened with an affection, which might in due course become something of permanence.

She lived in the Marais, a part of Paris which had been fashionable two centuries ago and was now undergoing a revival. Her apartment was in a new building which had been cleverly designed to fit in with the traditions of the old 17th-century houses and cloistered walks in and around the Place des Vosges. That she could afford such an apartment showed that she must be earning far more than he did, a fact which did not disturb him as it might many Frenchmen. So eminently practical, when they had slept together it had always been in her home rather than in his much more modest apartment or at an hotel.

Another reason which sharpened his anticipation was that while he was at the meeting of police chiefs, Ingrid had returned to Paris after spending a month in Rio de Janeiro on an assignment for the *Washington Post*. From there she had more than once telegraphed him in affectionate terms and told him how eagerly she looked forward to the evening they would spend together on her return. She used the word 'evening', but in a way that showed she meant night.

He told the driver of the fiacre to go directly to the Marais. They could easily have stopped at Sûreté headquarters on Quai des Orfèvres to leave his valise in his office for it was on the way, but he knew from experience that if he did he would find something there to detain him – a minor crisis or news of a crime that required his urgent attention. So the driver crossed the Seine further up river and headed for Place de la Bastille.

Ingrid's apartment was on the third floor of the building, but after he had paid the driver of the fiacre and was heading for the stairs, the concierge came out and held out an arm to stop him. Her eyes were swollen and red and he could see that she had been weeping.

'Madame Van de Velde is not there, Monsieur.' Gautier knew she had more to say, but could not find the words. He waited until she blurted them out. 'She is dead. She has been murdered.'

A policeman from the 4th arrondissement, who had been left on duty outside the entrance to Ingrid's apartment, gave him the facts. The concierge had found Ingrid's body soon after midday when she had taken up a packet which had been delivered for her. She had found Ingrid naked on her bed, apparently strangled. The police had been called as well as a doctor who had pronounced her dead. By that time it was considered too late to take the body to the mortuary, which would be done next morning when the inspector in charge of the case began his investigation. That was all the policeman was able to tell him.

Inside the apartment Gautier was aware that his brain was functioning in two separate ways. One part was trying incredulously to absorb the news he had been given; the other part was wrestling with the enormity of his loss, of grief and feelings of guilt. Had he not been at the meeting of police chiefs, he would have been in Paris the previous day when Ingrid had returned from abroad, he would have spent the evening with her that evening, slept with her that night and she would still be alive.

Ingrid's body lay on her bed where it had been found, but now covered with a sheet. Gautier had seen many dead bodies, perhaps too many he supposed, but as he pulled the sheet back he knew that he must be clinical, divorcing himself from all emotion. The first sight of a body could often give one an impression which might later prove to be invaluable in helping to solve the crime. He needed no medical knowledge to see that Ingrid had been strangled as well as stabbed, but there was surprisingly little blood on the sheets. In spite of that he concluded that she had first been stabbed. Strangling her may have been no more than an attempt to confuse, to disguise the identity of the killer. On the other hand it might equally have been done in an uncontrollable paroxysm of rage.

That posed the question of who could have murdered her. There was nothing to suggest that she might have been killed by an intruder. If she had had an enemy Gautier would have known about it. He was not ready to believe that she might have brought another lover home who might have killed her in a frenzy of lust.

The timing of her murder was also puzzling. Fluent in a number of languages, Ingrid was the Paris correspondent of the *Leipziger Volkszeitung* and also contributed columns to other newspapers, but she had had an ambition to work for the

Washington Post. On the strength of some articles she had written for the paper, she had been invited to meetings in Washington, following which she had been given a trial assignment for a month as a replacement for the paper's correspondent in Rio de Janeiro. If the trial was satisfactory, she had been told that she might expect to be given a correspondent's post somewhere in Europe, if not in Paris itself.

Now Gautier wondered whether she had been taken on by the *Washington Post* and if so, whether that might have led to her murder, though he could not see how. He went to the writing bureau which she had kept in the living room of the apartment and found it unlocked. That did not surprise him, for she had not been a secretive person, only a tidy one. In it he found only bills, receipts, letters from an aunt who lived in Rotterdam and other personal items. There were no letters from him, for he had never written her any, but he was touched to see that she had kept the one *petit bleu,* or message over Paris's pneumatic telegraph, which he had once sent her some weeks ago to confirm a meeting. Like most journalists she had rapidly become dependent on the telephone, using it and the telegraph as a means of daily, even hourly, communication.

In a waste-paper basket beside the writing bureau he found the torn-up remains of the steamer and train tickets for her journey back to France from Brazil. Beneath them were two leaflets, one announcing a sale of home furnishings and the other advertising a patent remedy for neuralgia, which must have been pushed through the letter-box of her apartment. As she had been away for a month, he was surprised there had not been many more. Beneath the tickets and leaflets lay an envelope which he picked up and examined. The way in which a woman opened an envelope could tell one much about her character and about what she may have expected it to contain. Ingrid had slit this one open carefully, no doubt with the paper-knife he had seen in the bureau, and had let it fall without its contents into the waste-paper basket. Gautier saw that it had been posted in Washington to her home address and would have arrived a few days before she reached Paris. He searched the bureau again, but could not find the letter it must have brought.

He had not expected to find much in the apartment connected with her work as a journalist, for although she wrote her longer articles and some of her columns at home, she had the use of an office in Rue Réaumur, which she shared with other journalists who wrote for foreign papers and which provided the facilities she needed. It was there that he might discover from her files and papers on what she had been working since her return to Paris and the names of anyone she might have contacted.

He pulled the sheet back over her and knew he would have to shut his mind to his last picture of her, and replace it with other pictures from the past; of her face, her infectious smile, her caresses and her naked body when they had made love. The bedroom was still as the concierge and the police must have found it. The following morning officers from the government scientific laboratories would come and examine the whole apartment, looking for anything which might tell them more about her death. Police forces had begun to use science as an aid to the detection of crime and the punishment of offenders, but little progress had yet been achieved and he felt it was unlikely that the scientists would find anything significant.

Two journalists were still at work in the office which Ingrid had shared with three others. That did not surprise him, for he knew that the publication of newspapers had become in many ways a nocturnal business. Even so, although he understood why those who produced daily newspapers in France might in the evenings wish to be looking for late news to print in the next morning's editions, he would not have thought that journalists working for foreign papers need be under the same constraint. On occasions when Ingrid had declined his invitation to dine with him, pleading work as an excuse, he had sometimes teased her for what he described as an affectation. She had laughed but had never taken him seriously.

Before going to Rue Réaumur, he had called in at the police commissariat in the 4th arrondissement and had been fortunate enough to catch the inspector who had been called to Ingrid's apartment when her body had been found, before he went off duty for the day. Inspector Mounier was a decent man and probably competent enough, but one could see that he had so far made little real effort in his investigations. Gautier realized that this was probably because he knew he would not be handling the case for long. This was no ordinary killing; not violence spilled over from the rough streets not far away, not the result of a quick knife thrust between *voyous* or pimps. The victim was a person of consequence and a foreigner and so the investigation would inevitably be taken over by the Sûreté. Mounier had clearly been impressed that an officer of Gautier's importance should be involved, but even so he had not been able to tell him more than he already knew, except that there had been no signs that whoever had murdered the lady had broken into her apartment.

Gautier's instructions to him were precise. The apartment should be guarded night and day and no one admitted until the official investigating team arrived. Ingrid's body should be re-examined by one of the doctors attached to the Sûreté and he should be told to look for evidence that she had been killed by stabbing. Attempts to make it appear as though she had been strangled might have been simply a device to conceal the truth.

He would expect the doctor's report to be on his desk by noon the next day.

He had previously met both of the two journalists whom he found at Ingrid's office. Luca Marinetti was a tall good-looking Italian and was listed as representing an Italian news agency as well as two other provincial newspapers. Pierre Bertrand was a Frenchman, quiet and polite, who acted as correspondent for some small English-language magazines and a medical journal. Neither man seemed surprised when Gautier arrived at the office, for he had called in there more than once in the evenings to meet Ingrid before they went out for dinner together. This evening one could tell from the way they welcomed him that they had not heard of Ingrid's death.

'Madame Van de Velde is not here,' Bertrand told him.

Gautier felt that there was no point in softening the news which he had to give them. 'I know Monsieur. I regret to tell you that she is dead.'

After a moment of shocked silence their questions flew at him. He gave them only the facts, for he had no wish to be drawn into speculation. Both men were clearly incredulous and Gautier found himself wondering how, if two seasoned journalists could not come to terms with Ingrid's death, he would ever be able to reconcile himself to it. He could not give them the luxury of time to recover their composure, for he had questions of his own to ask.

'Did Madame Van de Velde tell you that she might be leaving Paris?'

'You mean the assignment she was expecting from the Washington paper? Yes. She often talked of it.'

'Do you know if she had received any news of it when she returned from Brazil?'

'Yes. She told us a letter was waiting for her when she returned,' Bertrand said, 'but it was not the news which she had been expecting.'

'She was not offered a post?'

'Not an offer of a permanent position. Not yet. They wanted her to work in Berlin for three months on a temporary assignment, after which she would return and take over the Paris desk.'

'Paris? If that was definite it must have pleased her.'

'She was delighted. On the day when she had read the letter she could talk of very little else.'

Gautier could imagine how pleased and excited Ingrid must have been. Had she been offered a permanent post elsewhere in Europe she would have taken it, but reluctantly, for she loved working in Paris, which she often said was the cultural and intellectual centre of Europe. She had also made it clear that she had no wish to be separated from him.

'When was this?' he asked the two journalists.

'The day before yesterday which was the day she returned from Brazil.'

'Did she also come into your office yesterday?'

'She did and early, just as she would on a normal day.'

'Do you know if she had any appointments?'

'In the afternoon she went to a meeting arranged by the Ministry for Foreign Affairs,' Marinetti replied and then he added, 'Many of us in the foreign press corps went. I was there with her and our colleague Neuhoff, although in the event what they had to say did not amount to much; some minor diplomatic trouble with Germany. No doubt Madame Van de Velde had other meetings during the day, but she did not talk about them.'

'Do you know if she kept an appointments diary?'

'I am sure she did. When she was on the telephone I often heard her saying that she must consult her diary and then she would take it out of her desk.'

There were four desks in the office, one for each of the journalists who used the place. Each desk had a telephone on it and two drawers in which the journalists kept their notebooks, paper and personal belongings. Typewriters stood on some but not all of the desks, and Gautier remembered Ingrid often saying that she did not need one and could not be bothered to learn to type.

He knew which desk had been hers and went over to it. On it he saw a tray with pens in it, an inkwell, a blotter and nothing else. Ingrid had been a neat and careful person and she would have kept her diary in one of the drawers of the desk. Both drawers were open and there was no diary in either of them. He could see that the locks had not been forced and remembered then something which had escaped his attention when he had searched her apartment. The keys to the office and to her desk drawers had been missing.

'Did Ingrid keep her desk locked, do you know?' he asked the two men.

'Of course. We all do.' Bertrand shrugged his shoulders. 'You know how protective we journalists are of what we are writing and our sources.'

2

Next morning Gautier arrived at his office even earlier than he usually did, for he knew that work would have accumulated on his desk while he had been away at the meeting of police chiefs; not necessarily criminal cases but complaints, reports of missing persons, requests for investigations. Most of it would be tiresome and easy to delegate to other officials, but in almost all of it English and American visitors to Paris would be involved. He had been given sole responsibility for dealing with all police matters relating to Anglo-Saxon visitors, by the Director General of the Sûreté. Although he frequently complained about them, Courtrand admired the English, had his beard and moustaches modelled on those of King Edward and even sent his dress shirts to be laundered in London. Ever since the Entente Cordiale had been signed a few years ago, he had made it his mission to foster and encourage it, by making sure that the Sûreté gave a high priority to the safety and comfort of English and American visitors. Gautier was still also in charge of investigating major criminal cases, but he did not mind the extra work, for at least it was helping him to improve his command of the English language, which while improving was still far from fluent.

Today he had another reason for welcoming the extra load of work. The previous evening he had eaten alone and at a small café not far from Place des Vosges. His first inclination had been to dine as far as possible from where Ingrid had died, but he recognized that distance was not going to drive out the truth. Self-discipline and taxing work were what he would need if he were going to carry on with life and continue investigating Ingrid's murder calmly and without prejudice. Even so it had been a lonely dinner with a melancholy night to follow.

Now as soon as his principal assistant Surat arrived he sent for him. Surat had met Ingrid more than once, on occasions when the press had been brought in to the Sûreté and briefed on developments in a crime, and Gautier had always felt that he liked her. Now he was tactful enough, once he had been given the essential facts, not to begin asking questions. Gautier told him to go directly to the commissariat of the 4th arrondissement. Enough time had already been lost by Mounier's dilatory approach to the crime. Surat was to arrange for Ingrid's apartment to be searched again and thoroughly, and her concierge to be questioned as well as the other tenants of the apartment block. It was always possible that whoever had killed Ingrid might have been seen in the vicinity of the building on the evening of the murder.

'Our problem will be to learn more about Madame Van de Velde's movements and whether she might have met anyone in the hours before she was killed,' Gautier said. 'She had only been in Paris for two days after her return to this country.' He explained that he had already spoken to her journalist colleagues.

'Could it have been one of them who killed her?'

'It is unlikely, but later today I will be speaking to the other journalist who shared her office.'

After Surat had left, Gautier made a telephone call to the police in Rotterdam. Ingrid had told him that both her parents were dead and he never heard her mention any brothers or sisters. Her

18

former husband, he knew, had remarried and, he thought, was living in Vienna, so he had to assume that her aunt in Rotterdam was her nearest relative. After several minutes spent overcoming the habitual obstructiveness of the telephone operators, he eventually found himself speaking to a police officer of a similar rank to himself in Rotterdam. He was promised that the Dutch police would contact Ingrid's aunt at the address he had given them and inform her of her niece's death. If it seemed that she might know anything which could assist in the investigation, the Sûreté could send officers to Rotterdam to question her. Alternatively she might well be willing to travel to Paris to arrange for her niece's funeral and to wind up her affairs.

Gautier recognized that there was nothing more he could do for the time being. The problem which Ingrid's murder presented must be approached analytically. Very often in the successful solution of such cases there was an element of chance, the fortuitous discovery of a factor which would normally have passed unnoticed, a meeting or statement or even a remark which might easily have been overlooked. He would have to be patient and meanwhile he turned his attention once more to the reports which lay on his desk. They contained nothing of any great consequence. An American widow had been rash enough to accept an invitation to dine with a Frenchman whom she had met in the Louvre and when she returned to her hotel on the Left Bank she found that her room had been ransacked and her jewellery stolen. An English homosexual, while strolling in the Bois de Boulogne, had been attacked by two men and a third man who had intervened to help him, so he thought, had stolen his passport. A wealthy Irishman, in Paris to watch his horses race at Longchamps, had disappeared from his suite at the Hôtel Meurice. The cases were typical of those which he found waiting for him almost every morning when he arrived at Sûreté headquarters, and each would need action to be taken under his supervision until they were resolved.

On most mornings initiating the necessary action and taking care of the paperwork which resulted would take him until noon. Then if no major investigation intervened, he would go to the Café Corneille to take an aperitif before lunch. Today he was not in the mood for such distractions. Few of the friends whom he met at the café had known Ingrid and none would be aware of his relationship with her, but even so his sense of loss and lingering guilt would be inhibiting and prevent him enjoying their lively conversation and banter.

So he dispensed with lunch and worked through into the afternoon and when, soon after two, he was told that the Director General wished to see him, he was almost relieved. Courtrand was a trying individual, full of a sense of his own importance and very often petty and spiteful. His appointment had been political, a return for services which he had done on behalf of important people, but he knew that his successful administration of the Sûreté depended on the efforts of his subordinates. Today Gautier felt some sympathy for him, as the man had clearly not recovered fully from his indisposition, the Frenchman's typical *crise de foie*, difficult to define in medical terms, but not calculated to improve the temper.

'I am glad to know that you are in the office today,' he said as soon as Gautier arrived in his office, 'and not wasting your time and the resources of the department in some café.'

The gibe was unfair as well as petty, but Gautier was not going to show that he resented it. 'Monsieur?'

'The British Ambassador has asked if he might see me this afternoon in my office on a most delicate matter and I shall require you to be present.'

'Has he told you on what it is he needs your advice?'

'Yes. His daughter has been abducted.'

20

Gautier had never met Sir Donald Macnab, the British Ambassador in Paris, but he knew that he was a Scot and had the reputation of being well disposed towards the French. Certainly he had worked hard to cement the growing friendship between England and France, which many people now believed was essential to counter the growing threat of Prussian nationalism. Courtrand himself had insisted that the Sûreté should do everything in its power to establish good relations with the British Embassy. His senior officers were inclined to think he carried this policy too far, treating even minor embassy officials with a fawning respect. That Sir Donald had asked for an appointment with him, not at the embassy but in his office, suggested that he had a favour to ask.

That afternoon when Gautier went to Courtrand's office, Sir Donald was already there. He was a tall, lean man, a Highlander, Gautier supposed, because he had been told that people from the Lowland belt of Scotland were mostly short, sturdy and pugnacious. He was also not a man to spend time on social niceties for he began at once to talk of his concern for his daughter Fiona. She had left home early the previous morning and had not returned. It was only when Lady Donald had gone to her room and questioned the servants that they discovered she had taken with her a suitcase of clothes and her passport.

'What makes you believe she has been abducted, Sir Donald?' Courtrand asked.

'Friends of ours returning from England told us they had seen Fiona boarding the boat train at the Gare du Nord. She was in the company of a man whose name I understand is Walther Kossuth.'

'Might she not have eloped with him?'

Sir Donald made a gruff Scottish noise of contempt. 'Fiona is not an impressionable schoolgirl. She is thirty and to the best of my knowledge she has never had a romantic attachment or even a romantic thought in her life.'

'But surely, Sir Donald, do I not remember that she was once engaged?' Courtrand asked. He had always taken a close interest in the affairs of the diplomatic communities in Paris and particularly in those of the British embassy.

'That was years ago and it came to nothing.' One had the impression that Sir Donald had no wish to be reminded of his daughter's only romance.

'Does she have money, Sir Donald?' Gautier asked

Now they were talking of a subject which Sir Donald understood better than he understood the emotional susceptibilities of women. 'She has an allowance which I make her, pin money we call it back home, and as Fiona has always been a thrifty soul, she may have put a good bit away. But she has no money in her own right and will not have any until my wife or I die.'

'How can we help you, Sir Donald?' Courtrand asked.

'I am reluctant to ask this, Monsieur le Directeur, but I wondered whether you might be able to send one of your men over to England to find her. Simply to satisfy my wife and me that she has come to no harm.'

'Would it not be simpler to enlist the help of the British police?'

'That is out of the question. If we did and they found her, they might be obliged to bring charges. Then the Foreign Office would have to be involved. Besides, think of the scandal if it were known that she had left home with a man! We have relations in London. No, you French are so much better at handling affairs like this. You have the tact and the savoir-faire.'

'In that case, Sir Donald, I am sure something can be arranged.'

Gautier could see that Courtrand could not resist the compliments that were being paid to the Sûreté and therefore to himself.

Suddenly he realized why he had been asked to attend the meeting with Sir Donald. Only a few weeks previously he had been able to do the British Embassy in Paris a small service. Two elderly Scottish ladies had been picked up by the police helplessly drunk after foolishly allowing themselves to being persuaded to drink absinthe. Gautier had arranged for them to be released from prison swiftly without being charged and to be put on the first boat train to England. It had been hinted that the two ladies might have been distant relatives of Sir Donald.

'Have you any idea, Monsieur L'Ambassadeur, what this man with whom your daughter is travelling does for a living?' He felt he could ask the question now that any pretence that Sir Donald's daughter had been abducted had been tacitly dropped.

Sir Donald ignored the question. 'My wife saw her dancing at a recent ball with this Kossuth. All we know of him is that he is a plausible rogue and she was told that he had entered the country on a false passport.'

'Has he been to your residence?'

'Never, at least not as far as I know.'

'Could we speak to Lady Macnab about it?'

'I would prefer it if you did not. She knows no more about the man than I do and she really is most upset by my daughter's absence. Why do you not speak with our servants? Servants as you know are very inquisitive and they gossip among themselves endlessly.'

'I will arrange for that to be done, Sir Donald,' Courtrand said.

'But please on no account mention the reason for my coming here this morning to any of the embassy staff. At this point I would prefer it that they know nothing of the matter.'

They discussed what might be done about the disappearance of Sir Donald's daughter a little longer, but only in general terms. Sir Donald agreed that he would give Courtrand the names of two families who might be contacted, one in London and one in Scotland, but only in an emergency. Both were families whom his daughter might approach if she found herself in difficulties. His secretary, he said, would type out the names and addresses of both families and have them sent round to Sûreté headquarters by messenger within an hour.

'Well, Gautier,' Courtrand said after the ambassador had left, 'as you can see, my policy of cultivating good relations with the British Embassy has been justified. We can be proud that Sir Donald has entrusted us with this delicate mission.'

'You do not find this whole business rather odd, Monsieur?'

'Odd? In what way?'

'From what we have been told, it is obvious that his daughter has not been abducted.'

'If Sir Donald says she has been, we must accept his word for that.'

'Could it be that he is merely trying to save face? That she has just left home with a man and perhaps after a quarrel with her parents?'

'I cannot understand why you are taking such a negative view. You are always so suspicious, Gautier.'

Gautier might have told him that suspicion was, or should be, an essential weapon in the armoury of a police officer, but he knew that would achieve nothing. So he asked Courtrand a question, to which he already had guessed the answer. 'Then who are we to send to England?'

'You, of course! I cannot spare anyone else.'

Back in his office Gautier recognized that at any other time he would have welcomed an opportunity of visiting England. He had been to London only once some years previously, also on Sûreté business, and although investigating a crime could never be enjoyable, he had found the experience stimulating. Now however he felt that all his attention should be concentrated on finding out who had murdered Ingrid. Ridiculous though it might seem, leaving Paris in pursuit of a young women who had left the country in the company of a man, seemed almost like a betrayal, adding to the guilt he already felt. Even so he knew he had no alternative except to obey Courtrand's instructions, and all he could do in the few hours left to him in Paris was to make sure that the investigation into Ingrid's death was being properly conducted so that he could take it under control on his return.

He did not expect to be away for more than two or three days at the most. Sir Donald's daughter had made little effort to conceal the fact that she was leaving Paris for England and he did not suppose it would be too difficult to discover where she and the man she was with had gone after they had crossed the channel. Soon after he had returned to his office, the second medical report on Ingrid's body was brought to him. As he had expected this showed that a stab to the heart had been the cause of death. The bruises on her throat, the swelling and the congestion of blood in the dead woman's face had all been part of a clumsy attempt made immediately after she had been stabbed, to suggest that she had died of strangulation. In the second search of the bedroom carried out that morning the ligature used for the deception, the cord of Ingrid's dressing gown, had been found under the bed.

While he was reading the report Surat came into his office. Surat was a conscientious police officer, no longer young, who had somehow been passed over for promotion. He was also loyal to Gautier – perhaps too loyal. He had spent much of the morning talking with the concierge who had first told Gautier of Ingrid's death, as well as to other tenants of the building and some of their servants. No one, he told Gautier, had seen anyone loitering in the vicinity, nor any strangers in the corridors or on the stairs of the building.

'The concierge insists that she has never seen any louts near the building; the district is too exclusive, but I would not believe everything she says.'

'Why do you think that?'

'Like many widowed concierges she finds the long evening hours lonely and looks for companionship in wine.'

Gautier was prepared to believe him. In a number of the murders on which they had worked together concierges had been key witnesses, and Surat had developed his own method of dealing with them. If there was any information to be had from the concierge or from the servants of the other tenants in the building, he would unearth it in due course. Gautier told him that he would be leaving for England next morning on the first boat train and together they drew up a list of what was to be done while he was away. Before then he wished to speak with Ingrid's other fellow journalists and, leaving the Sûreté, they found a fiacre to take them to Rue Réaumur. On the way he told Surat of his visit to the office the previous day, of his conversations with Bertrand and Marinetti and of how they had been unable to suggest any reason why Ingrid had been murdered nor knew of any enemies she might have had. Surat may well have known that Ingrid had been working in Rio de Janeiro, but Gautier did not tell him that she had since been offered a post outside Paris, as that might only add complications to the instructions he was going to give him.

'In spite of what the concierge says, could Madame Van de Velde not have been attacked by a thief?' Surat asked.

'As far as I could tell nothing was stolen. The jewellery she had been wearing was still lying there. And the door to the apartment had apparently not been forced.'

26

'You believe she may have admitted her killer to the apartment?'

'She may have met him somewhere in the city during the evening and he followed her home.' Gautier wondered why he could not bring himself to believe that Ingrid might have dined with the man and then invited him back to her apartment. 'We cannot check on that because her appointments diary is missing.'

'Have you any idea why?'

'The name of the man who killed her might have been in it. In that case he would have taken it with him, as well as the keys to her desk at the office.'

When they reached Rue Réaumur they found only one journalist and he had not been there at the time of Gautier's first visit. His name was Neuhoff, a native of Alsace who represented both German and Belgian newspapers. He had already been told of Ingrid's murder and indeed by that time the news would have reached most of the journalists in Paris.

'My condolences, Inspector,' he said as he shook Gautier's hand. 'I cannot imagine who would have wished to kill Madame Van de Velde. She was such a charming colleague, so gifted and so sympathetic.'

'We are hoping you may be able to assist us in identifying whoever it was.'

Gautier explained that Ingrid's diary was missing and that he wondered whether Neuhoff might have heard her mention any names while she had been in the office on the day of her death, or even making an appointment over the telephone.

Neuhoff shook his head. 'She scarcely used the telephone all day, but that may have been because she had been away from Paris and had only just returned.'

'Did she leave the office at all?'

'Only when she and I went together to a meeting for the press arranged by the Ministry for Foreign Affairs.'

'Did you see her speaking to anyone at the meeting?'

'No one in particular, though now that you mention it, I noticed that she did have a long conversation with a man there. I assume he was a journalist.'

'You do not know this man?'

'No, but I think he must have been a foreigner. He and Madame Van de Velde were not speaking French.'

'What language were they speaking then? German? I understand the meeting was about a political incident with Germany.'

'No, if it had been German I would have understood what they were saying; or Italian or Spanish.'

'You have no idea what it was?'

'I can only guess. By the sound of it I suspect it may have been one of the Balkan languages.'

'As far as you know she did not leave the meeting with anyone?

'No. I myself left early for I had a train to catch for Strasbourg. My old mother was celebrating her birthday.'

When they left Rue Réamur, Gautier told Surat go by fiacre to the Ministry for Foreign Affairs. The Minister and other politicians would have left for their homes by now, but the civil servants would still be at their desks. He was to ask them to let him have a list of everyone who had been invited to the meeting which Ingrid and Neuhoff had attended. He did not know how such meetings were arranged and whether a note was kept of all those who were present, but it was worth asking. Gautier himself set out on foot for the Place des Vosges.

Returning to Ingrid's apartment was something he would have preferred to have avoided. He had no wish to face its emptiness and its many reminders of Ingrid's personality and her sensual appeal. But he realized that he must overcome his reluctance, if he were to master the even more harrowing emotions which would lie ahead before the murderer could be identified; emotions of anger, revulsion and loathing.

A policeman was still on duty, stationed outside the door to Ingrid's apartment. Once he had been admitted to the apartment, he went straight to Ingrid's writing bureau. He saw there were papers in it which he had not examined closely on his last visit. Among copies of correspondence with the other papers to whom she had contributed, he found the document which he hoped he might find there. It was her curriculum vitae and gave details not only of the positions she had held in journalism, but of her upbringing and education. He supposed it was a copy of the document which she sent to Washington.

He already knew that Ingrid had been born and educated in Holland and that after taking her university degree, she had worked as a journalist in Brussels as well as Vienna and Paris. Her marriage to a Frenchman had lasted for only three years, but she had not told Gautier and he had never thought to ask, that her husband had been a member of the French diplomatic corps, who for a time had held a posting in Vienna. The languages in which Ingrid had been fluent were listed at the end of her curriculum vitae and as well as French, German, English, Italian and Spanish, they included Serbo-Croat.

3

Next morning the weather over the Channel was invigorating, with a fresh south-westerly wind, strong enough to make the sea choppy, but not uncomfortably rough for the passengers on the cross-channel steamer. As he walked along the promenade deck, Gautier tried to shake off the irritation he felt at having to leave Paris on a trivial quest in pursuit of a diplomat's daughter who, he felt certain, had left home of her own volition. The more important question of why and by whom Ingrid had been murdered remained unanswered and might well do until he returned.

In the meantime he must decide what he would do when he reached London. All he knew about Sir Donald's daughter Fiona, was that she was unmarried and about thirty years of age. The previous evening he had gone round to the offices of *Le Figaro*, the paper for which one of his closest friends worked, and after searching through files of press cuttings, found a photograph of Miss Macnab taken at a society ball a year or two previously, in which she had been standing between her father and mother. He also had the addresses of two families, one living in London and one in Scotland to whom, Sir Donald thought, she might turn if she found herself in difficulties.

They were meagre resources on which to undertake the errand on which he had been sent, but Gautier was not discouraged. Some years ago he had been to London to carry out enquiries related to the murder of an English woman in Paris. He had managed largely because of the help he had been given by Madame Régine, a former French actress, who was running a theatrical boarding house in Camden Town. On this trip he would not be lodging at her establishment, since he felt that he needed to stay somewhere nearer to London's social centre and the Sûreté had booked him a room in a modest hotel in Bloomsbury. Even so he was sure that if he needed help he could turn to Madame Régine.

Sir Donald Macnab had been curiously reticent in giving information about the man whom he claimed had abducted his daughter. Gautier wondered whether this may have been because she had left home willingly and with someone who was considered unsuitable, a notorious philanderer or gigolo, and her father was trying to protect his family from scandal. If this were true, there was at least a chance that the man might be known in the *demi-monde* of Paris, in which Madame Régine still had connections. That would at least give him a starting point for his enquiries.

When the steamer docked in Dover, he went to board the train to London which was waiting at the station. There had not been many passengers on a voyage which had left Paris so early and he found a seat in an empty compartment. The train appeared to be in no hurry to depart and this only fuelled the impatience Gautier had felt ever since leaving Paris. Presently two women came into the compartment. They must have been people of some importance, for they were conducted to their seats by an official in uniform, presumably the station master. He glanced at Gautier, wondering perhaps whether he should ask him to leave and find a seat elsewhere, so that the two ladies might be left on their own. Then he must have thought better of it and instead began assuring the women that their heavy luggage had been stowed safely in the guard's van and that it would be made available for them as soon as the train reached London.

Once he had left, the two women, who had been conversing with him in English, began talking to each other in French. One could see that they were both French, a mother and daughter in all probability, and they were discussing family matters; in particular the behaviour of the younger woman's husband, the fact that he had never once telephoned her while she was in France and whether he would be there to meet them when the train arrived in London. Either they were not aware that Gautier could understand their conversation or did not care.

The younger woman was carrying a small valise, not much larger than a handbag, attached to which was a luggage label carrying the name 'Mme O. Crespelle'. Seeing it Gautier remembered that Crespelle was the name of Ingrid's former husband. Immediately he wondered whether this might be a remarkable coincidence. Crespelle was an unusual name. Could he be travelling on the same train as the woman whom Ingrid's husband had married after his divorce? Crespelle, he knew, had been in the French foreign service. If his wife was in possession of a diplomatic passport that would explain the attention she was being given on her voyage. Shamelessly he listened to the conversation of the two women all the way to London, but was given no other clues which might confirm his suspicions, except a marginal one, another name. The younger of the women referred to her husband as 'Philippe'. On the rare occasions when she mentioned her ex-husband, Ingrid had also used that name.

When the train arrived in London no husband was there to meet them, only a chauffeur with an automobile, in which they were driven, stiff-faced to whatever welcome might be waiting for them. As he made his way by tramcar to Bloomsbury, Gautier wondered whether, when attempting to inform Ingrid's next-of-kin of her death, he should not have also tried to trace Philippe Crespelle. Then he decided that this must be a family matter and not an official obligation. If Ingrid's aunt in Rotterdam thought that Crespelle should be notified, she would no doubt contact him.

The hotel in which he was to stay was adequate enough, his room functional and neat. He could not help feeling though that the whole place was almost oppressively clean, smelling of polish and a hint of disinfectant. A French hotel of similar standing might not be so hygienic but it would offer little comforting touches to make the lodger feel more at home. By the time he had installed himself and unpacked his valise it was early evening, so he found a hansom cab to drive him to Madame Régine's boarding house in Camden Town. When he reached it he met an unexpected set-back. Madame Régine was no longer the owner. Ill-health had forced her to sell the place and she had returned to her family's home in Deauville. The new owner, also a middle-aged woman, was not French and although she was obliging enough, Gautier soon realized that she would be unable to help him.

Prudently he had kept the driver of the hansom cab waiting so he had himself driven to the Essex music hall in Islington where, at the time of his last visit to London, a French artiste had been singing naughty songs under the name of Mimi la Belle. Mimi had also been a great help to him and he taken her to supper at Romano's restaurant. His slender hope that she might still be per-forming at the Essex was not fulfilled and no one at the music hall had any news or even any knowledge of her. The careers of per-formers in the music halls, he realized, were as volatile and unpredictable as the performers themselves.

On his previous visit to London, Madame Régine had also taken him to a public house called The Running Footman. In one way the place was aptly named, for a large proportion of those who used it were servants from the large households of the gentry in and around Mayfair. Now he went there again, more through lack of any ideas of what else he should do than from any expectation that he might learn anything there about Sir Donald's daughter. Not wishing to appear conspicuous, he ordered a quart pot of porter, the dark beer which the majority of the men in the place were drinking. The women, many of them stout and elderly, were mostly drinking gin.

He did not enjoy the porter, finding it too heavy for his taste and he knew from experience that the gin sold in England was fiery and immature. Whisky, he supposed, would be the drink of men in England, and without finishing the porter he decided he would switch to a whisky, after which he would leave the tavern, have a meal and then return to his hotel. Starting his attempts to trace Miss Macnab and her abductor would have to wait until the morning. When he ordered a whisky, he tried asking the tap man who was pouring it for directions to a café, but his command of English could not have been as good as he believed, for the man did not understand him. Fortunately a young woman sitting nearby did and decided to come to his aid.

She said to Gautier in French, 'Are you by any chance French, Monsieur?'

'I am, Mademoiselle. How did you know?'

'Your English accent, Monsieur. It is even worse than mine.' The woman smiled. 'I am from France too. Is this your first evening in London? Perhaps I can help you.'

Gautier knew that London had its share of women of easy virtue, who could be found in the music halls, the taverns and the streets, at least as many as there were in Paris, but he felt certain that this young woman could not be a *putain*. She was too stylishly dressed and too well spoken. He thanked her for her offer

35

of help and she told him that there were few cafés in that neighbourhood, which was mainly residential and that he would do
better to look for one in Soho, which was only a short walk away.

'May I ask, Mademoiselle, do you live here?' Gautier was certain that she would not think his question impertinent.

'No, I have an apartment in Kensington. I come here quite
often to meet my sister. She is a children's governess to a family
in Park Street.'

'And you, Mademoiselle? Are you a governess too?'

'No, a secretary. I work in the French Embassy. And you,
Monsieur?'

Gautier smiled. 'If I had told you at the outset, you would
probably not be speaking to me now. I am a policeman.'

'A flic? I have no reason to fear the flics.'

'I would hope not! A charming young woman like you!'

He told her that he was a little more than an ordinary policeman;
that he was an inspector with the Sûreté in Paris. She told him that
her name was Sylvie Lambert, that she had been working in London
for almost three years and that her family came from the Dordogne.
Had she come from Paris, she might well have heard of him. He
was glad that she had the tact not to ask him what he was doing in
London; not because he had any objection to telling her, but it was
unlikely that she would be able to help him to trace Miss Macnab
and he preferred to chat with her on friendly, social matters.

He saw that she was drinking cognac. At home in France she
would no doubt be drinking wine, but she had probably concluded that The Running Footman had no wine worth drinking, nor
any of the recognized aperitifs which young women in France
would usually prefer. When her glass was almost empty and he
offered another cognac, she declined.

'I must be going,' she said. 'My sister is obviously not coming
to meet me this evening. Sometimes she finds it difficult to get

36

away from her duties with the children at this hour.'

'I hope, Mademoiselle, that you will not take this suggestion amiss, but would you be willing to come and dine with me?' Gautier knew that he might well be rebuffed, but he had decided the chance was worth taking. He continued, smiling, 'As you can see I am lost here, helpless in this Anglo-Saxon jungle, so could you not see your way to rescuing me, if only through patriotism?'

Sylvie laughed. 'Now I know I am with a Frenchman! What a gallant invitation!'

'Then you will join me?'

'Why not? If one cannot trust a policeman, whom can one trust?'

The restaurant where they dined was obviously modelled on one of the many French cafés on the Left Bank of Paris. The food was good and so was the wine, although in Gautier's view the price charged for it was monstrous. Sylvie had a sense of humour and he had difficulty in matching the amusing stories she painted of her life in London. He had invited her to dine with him simply for the pleasure of her company, so he did not tell her why he had come to London. In any case at that point it had not occurred to him that she would be able to help him in any way.

'You cannot imagine,' Sylvie said presently. 'what a pleasure it is to be spending an evening with a Frenchman.'

'You do not care for the English?'

'I have learnt to live with them, but I cannot pretend that I enjoy their company.'

'But one presumes that your colleagues at the French Embassy are mainly French?'

'They are of course, but – how can I put it? – after a time here in England they all seem to lose their French gaiety of spirit. They become defensive and dull, little island strongholds in a foreign sea. And at the same time they grow isolated and mistrustful even of other French people.'

The mention of the French Embassy in London reminded Gautier of the conversation he had overheard in the train from Dover. He decided it could do no harm to ask Sylvie, whether the couple on the train might be known to the French Embassy.

'Is there by any chance a diplomat named Crespelle on the staff of your mission?' he asked her.

'There is. Philippe Crespelle. Why, do you know him?'

'We have never met but I knew his first wife, Ingrid Van de Velde.'

'She is from Holland, is she not? He sometimes talks of her.'

'He may not know that she is dead.'

'I am certain he does not. How dreadful!'

'Her next-of-kin, an aunt in Rotterdam, has been informed of her death. The authorities did not know where they could contact her former husband.'

Sylvie looked at him, but did not ask Gautier the obvious question, although she must have realized that if the Sûreté was involved, Ingrid's death must have been in some way connected with violence. He was grateful for her tact, for even a mention of murder might spoil an evening which, he sensed, Sylvie was enjoying. So he did not ask her any more questions about Crespelle, but they talked of other things: of life in Paris, of the plays that were being performed, of Lucien Guitry and Sarah Bernhardt and other leading actors, of politics and society and incidents that had made headlines in the newspapers.

After they had finished eating and lingering over coffee, Gautier insisted on taking Sylvie to her lodgings in Kensington in a hansom cab. When they reached them he did not expect that she would invite him in to join him in a final glass of cognac or port and she did not. She was a respectable young woman, *bien élevée* as the French would say, who might have dined with a man she did not know, but in exceptional circumstances and because both of them were in a foreign land.

On her doorstep she looked at him and asked, 'Were you thinking that you should inform Monsieur Crespelle of the death of his first wife?'

'Now that I know where he is living I can arrange for the Sûreté to write and inform him officially, unless of course you feel he might prefer to be told in person.'

'Why not, while you are here in London? I do not know the circumstances of her death, but I believe he would take it as a kindness.'

'Could you arrange for me to meet him?'

'Certainly I can, if you come to the Embassy tomorrow morning?'

In the end Gautier agreed that he would call at the French Embassy the following morning at half past ten. Sylvie would by then have arranged an appointment for him with Crespelle as soon as possible afterwards. As he was being driven back to his hotel, Gautier admitted to himself that one of his motives for wishing to see Ingrid's former husband was no more than curiosity. Ingrid had sometimes spoken of him, but never in anger nor even with regret. She had given the impression that she believed they were incompatible and should never have married. Now he would be able to judge for himself.

At the same time he had another motive. He had a feeling that his chance meeting with Sylvie might in some way be turned to his advantage in his search for Fiona Macnab. Sir Donald had made it clear that he did not want the staff of the British Embassy in Paris, nor the authorities in London, to be told of his daughter's abduction or elopement or whatever he chose to call it, but instinct told Gautier that the French Embassy in London might be able to help him. The French were better than the English at dealing with problems which arose between people of opposite sex. It was not that they were more romantic or even more cynical, but as Sir Donald himself had said, Frenchmen seemed to have an instinctive flair for understanding the subtleties of relationships between man and woman.

'I will look forward to seeing you tomorrow morning then,' he told Sylvie as he kissed her hand.

Philippe Crespelle was tall and good-looking and had a self-assurance which bordered on arrogance. When Gautier saw him in his office the following morning and explained that he had come to inform him of the death of Ingrid Van de Velde, Crespelle was clearly astonished. She must have been much the same age as he was.

'So young! How did she die?'

'I regret so say we found her dead in her apartment. She had been murdered.'

Crespelle accepted the news as any diplomat would, without obvious emotion.

'Who could possibly have wished to kill her? Ingrid was a good person. I cannot ever remember her saying anything malicious or spiteful about anyone.'

Gautier might have agreed, but he did not wish to give the man even a hint of what his relationship with Ingrid had been. That might come later. 'Have you arrested anyone?' Crespelle asked.

'Not as yet.'

'But you have a suspect?'

'Not really. As you yourself said, Mademoiselle Van de Velde was a popular person with many friends and did not appear to have had any obvious enemies.'

'She was using her family name then?'

The knowledge that Ingrid had reverted to her maiden name

after their divorce seemed to offend Crespelle. He may have thought that as he had given his name to a woman, she should have continued to use it even after they separated, if only through respect.

'The two of you lived in Vienna for a time, I understand,' Gautier remarked.

'Yes, I was with the embassy there. In fact it was in Vienna that our marriage began to founder,' Crespelle said. He went on to explain, 'For a diplomat's wife to have her own career always creates problems. You see she has an active role to play in the life of the mission, giving her husband essential support and often there is a conflict between her duty as a journalist and the policy the embassy is following.'

Gautier could appreciate what Crespelle was saying. A successful journalist had to be inquisitive, to scratch below the surface and sometimes to unmask policies which those who made them would prefer to have concealed. 'Did Mademoiselle Van de Velde make any friend among the journalists in Vienna?' he asked Crespelle.

Crespelle looked at him sharply. 'Why do you ask that?'

'We have been told that she had a long conversation with a journalist, possibly a Croat, at a meeting of the press in Paris on the afternoon before she was murdered. It may not amount to anything, but it is the only possible lead we have been given.'

Crespelle took his time before he answered Gautier's question. 'I shall tell you this in case it may be helpful. In Vienna she struck up a friendship with a journalist named Igor Andrassy. I am sure there was nothing sinister in it. They were working on stories together, that is all, but at one point we were sufficiently concerned about Andrassy to have the man watched.'

'Was there any special reason for that?'

'Nothing one could put one's finger on. He was too immersed

in the politics of Austro-Hungary and I am afraid Ingrid allowed herself to become involved as well. They became convinced that agitators were trying to promote war fever in the Balkans and so to bring Austria in to any conflict on the side of Germany. As you know diplomats must remain neutral and Ingrid's intrigues became an embarrassment to us.'

'Intrigues?'

'That may be too strong a word, but they used to mingle with dissident groups in cafés. They used to joke quite openly about a sinister individual they had never identified, but whom they had christened BB.'

'What did the initials stand for?'

Crespelle shrugged. 'Ingrid never told me and I never bothered to ask. "Butcher of the Balkans" I suspect. In my opinion it was all very juvenile.'

They talked for a little longer, but about other more general matters, and Gautier formed the impression that Crespelle might be beginning to regret having told him about Ingrid's activities in Vienna. Even so when the time came for him to leave, Crespelle shook his hand warmly. One sensed that he still thought of Ingrid with affection and, remembering the conversation he had over-heard on the train journey from Dover to London, Gautier wondered whether he might be finding life less comfortable with his second wife and mother-in-law.

When Sylvie Lambert came to escort Gautier out of the embassy, Crespelle said, 'Mind you catch the scoundrel who killed Ingrid, Inspector.'

'I am sure we will.'

As they were walking along a corridor Sylvie said to Gautier, 'Now that you have spoken to Monsieur Crespelle, I suppose you will be returning to Paris.'

'Not immediately. That was only one of the reasons for my visit.'

He explained that he had also come to England to see if he could trace the movements of a diplomat's daughter and to reassure himself that she was safe and well. He told Sylvie of the constraints that Sir Donald Macnab had imposed on any enquiries he might make about Fiona. When she asked him how he thought he might trace her, he had to admit that he had not yet planned how to go about it. The only thought he had was that Fiona might have a diplomatic passport, and as such might well be given favourable treatment when she entered the country. He remembered the deference which the authorities had paid to Madame Crespelle and her mother at Dover.

He explained what he had in mind to Sylvie. 'The passport people might well remember Mademoiselle Macnab and they may have asked where she planned to stay while she was in England.'

'That is more than likely. In which case I may be able to help you.'

'In what way?'

'We work very closely with the English authorities over questions of securing entry to the country for French nationals and the immigration regulations. If you wish I could have a word with my contacts there.'

'I could not possibly put you to so much trouble.'

'It will be no trouble. I am busy this morning, but I will raise the matter with the English passport people this afternoon.'

Gautier gave her a rough description of Fiona Macnab from what he remembered, having seen her once or twice at social occasions in Paris and from the photograph of her he had found in *Le Figaro*. She was slim and tall, he recalled, with no particular outstanding features, apart from her nose which was slightly hooked in the style of the British aristocracy. She had given the impression not of having a forceful personality, but of carrying that permanent look of diffidence associated with young people brought up by strict, demanding parents. He also told Sylvie that Fiona had probably been travelling with a man who might not be a French national, possibly a Hungarian.

'Shall I come to see you this afternoon,' he concluded, 'so you can tell me what you have been able to find out?'

'No. It would be better if we met later this evening; perhaps in the Running Footman at, shall we say, half past six?'

After leaving the French Embassy Gautier spent the afternoon learning a little more about London. He visited museums, an art gallery, stared at the palaces of royalty and walked in public parks. There was nothing else he could usefully do, for he was confident that the enquiries that Sylvie Lambert was making represented the best hope of finding Fiona Macnab. Even so he could not help wondering whether she had agreed to tell him anything she might learn that evening simply so that he might take her out to dinner again. There was nothing wrong in that. They had both enjoyed dining in Soho and there was no reason why they should not do so again. He was fortunate to have found a young lady who was prepared to work on his behalf and for such a modest reward.

Later in the afternoon when he returned to his hotel in Bloomsbury, he found a telegram from Surat waiting for him. It told Gautier simply that the journalist to whom Ingrid had been speaking at the meeting in the Ministry for Foreign Affairs had been identified. He was a Magyar named Igor Andrassy, well respected in Austria and said to be an authority on the affairs of the Empire.

When at a few minutes after six Sylvie came into The Running Footman, he could tell at once that she had news for him. After he had bought her a cognac and they were sitting down together, she told him, 'Your Mademoiselle Macnab is in Scotland. She and her friend booked in to a small hotel in Edinburgh.'

'Does this mean that the authorities are checking on her movements?'

'Not hers, her friend's. You were right, he is Hungarian; a man named Walther Kossuth, one of a group of agitators who we believe have been stirring up trouble in the Balkans.'

'Will you join me for dinner and you can tell me all about it?'

'No, I am sorry Inspector but I already have a dinner engagement.' Sylvie opened a file she was carrying and handed him a sheet of notepaper. 'There is the name of the hotel where they are staying and below it are the names of some other hotels where you may wish to stay. I assume you will not wish to book in at the same hotel as them.'

'You are right. How do I get to Edinburgh? By railway?'

'Yes. There is an overnight train which leaves at eight tonight.' She opened her file again and handed him more papers. 'I took the liberty of getting you a ticket for the journey and also a berth in the sleeping car.' She smiled. 'I do not picture you as a man who would enjoy sitting up all night.'

Impressed by her efficiency, Gautier took the papers and tickets and took out his wallet to repay what she had spent. 'Thank you for all you have done, Mademoiselle. I hope that when I am passing through London on my way back to Paris, you will allow me to take you out to dinner.'

Sylvie smiled. 'I would never forgive you if you did not.'

4

Gautier's hotel in Edinburgh was in the north of the city, an area known to local people as Morningside. He had chosen it from the list of hotels which Sylvie Lambert had given him, not because it was in a residential district that was supposed to be fashionable, but because it was some distance from the hotel where Fiona Macnab was staying. At some point, he supposed, he would have to approach Miss Macnab, find out whether she was safe and in good hands and tell her of her father's concern. For the time being though he would only try to keep an eye on her, watch her movements and then decide whether she would welcome any intervention from him.

He had never met Miss Macnab formally, but she may well have seen him at social functions in Paris, and he could not rule out the possibility that she might recognize him if she saw him in the streets around her hotel. If she did and realized that she was under surveillance, she and her companion might take fright and leave Edinburgh. It was only by good fortune that he had been able to track her to Scotland and if they fled, he could not expect to find anyone as helpful and efficient as Sylvie Lambert to help him follow them again.

In the afternoon of his first full day in Edinburgh, after registering at his hotel, he went on foot across the city towards where

Miss Macnab was staying. To do so he had to pass the centre of Edinburgh, with its fine streets and imposing buildings. Many of the names he saw – Princes Street, George Street, Charlotte Square – appeared to be associated with the English royal family. Gautier found that surprising, for he had always understood that the Scots as a race were fiercely independent and still resented that arbitrary act which had united the two countries and made them subject to governance by a Hanovarian dynasty.

When he had identified the position of the Killiecrankie Hotel in which Miss Macnab was supposed to be staying, he took up a position some distance away from where he could watch its entrance. He waited and watched for more than an hour, moving every few minutes to another vantage point. From time to time people went into and came out of the hotel, but none of them had any resemblance to Miss Macnab. Eventually he came to the conclusion he could spend his time more effectively. Fiona Macnab and her companion could not stay in the Killiecrankie indefinitely. They would have to come out, if only to have a meal.

Evening was approaching so he abandoned his vigil and went in search of any cafés that might be close to the hotel. He found one, but it was such a mean, inhospitable place that he could not imagine the daughter of a diplomat and one used to the style and elegance of even the most humble French café, agreeing to enter it. A few metres from the café there was a bar which seemed altogether superior in appearance, with wood panelled walls and electric lamps. Gautier could think of few ordinary bars in Paris which had by then replaced gas lighting with electricity. Reproductions of two large oil paintings hung in the bar: one of a full-length figure of a proud elderly man in full highland dress, a clan chief perhaps; the other of a stag with a magnificent head and antlers held high defiantly.

Although he felt it was unlikely that Miss Macnab and her companion might go into that particular bar, he decided he would take a drink there. Apart from anything else, by spending some time in the bar he might get a feel for social life in Edinburgh, which would help him form an idea of why the couple had come to the city. He could see that the majority of people in the place were drinking whisky so he ordered a glass himself. Many of the customers drank standing up by the bar counter or in groups around the room, a habit of which he had always disapproved. Drinking should not be an end to itself, but a social accompaniment to leisure, to be enjoyed in comfort.

Against one of the walls of the room was a wooden bench, so he went and sat there as he sipped his whisky. He had not really enjoyed the whisky he had drunk at The Running Footman in London, finding it too fiery for his taste. The one he was given here was much smoother, with a rich flavour not unlike that of Armagnac.

Two men were sitting a little way along from him on the bench. The reason they were sitting may have been that one of them appeared to be partially crippled. They were talking about whisky, indignantly, complaining about a Royal Commission that had been set up by the government in London, to enquire into the true nature of whisky and in what ways it might be distilled. As far as the two men sitting near Gautier were concerned, there was only one true whisky – malt whisky, made in the traditional distilleries in the Highlands and Islands of Scotland. All Scots knew that. Whisky was their national drink and there was no need for Royal Commissions to tell them how it should be made.

'It is essential that the reputation and quality of whisky should be protected,' one of the men said, 'now that people are beginning to drink it in other countries. It could become a valuable export.'

'Surely not much is being sold abroad?'

'Not much now, maybe, but it will grow. Only yesterday an American came into our bank wanting to change dollars into British currency. He said he needed the money to purchase whisky which he wished to have shipped out to the restaurant which he owns in New York.'

The man's remark set Gautier thinking. He remembered Sir Donald Macnab saying that his daughter was a thrifty girl and might have saved money out of her allowance. 'Put a good bit away' was the expression he had used. If she had done that surely she would have brought the money with her when she left home. The allowance would have been paid to her in French money and after she crossed the channel she would have had to have it changed. The couple would be in a hurry to avoid pursuit and it was reasonable to suppose that Fiona would have postponed changing her money until she reached Scotland. That gave him an idea.

Next morning he crossed over from Morningside and in Queen Street found what must be nearest bank to the Killiecrankie Hotel. He waited until the bank opened for business and then instead of waiting on the off-chance that Fiona Macnab might appear to use it, he went in himself. He had changed enough money in London for his immediate expenses, but he still had some French francs left. There was only one teller in the bank and handing him the francs, Gautier asked for them to be changed into British currency.

While the teller was making his calculations, he remarked, 'I imagine you do not often see French money here.'

'Not often,' the teller replied and then he smiled as he added, 'The Auld Alliance between your country and ours is not as solid as it once was.'

Gautier knew he was talking about the alliance between France and Scotland which dated back hundreds of years ago. Seeing that the man was not averse to conversation, he tried another approach. 'A friend of mine, a Scottish lady, advised me to use your bank. She said you were very helpful the other day when she came here to change her French money.'

'That would be Miss Macnab. Yes, we were able to assist her.'

'She told me she would be staying in the Killiecrankie Hotel. Do you know by any chance if she is still there?'

The teller's expression changed. He did not reply to the question but it was clear that he had something he would like to say. There was another customer waiting behind Gautier, so he said, 'Would you mind if I deal with this customer, sir?' He took some cheques and cash which the customer wanted paid in and then when they were alone he asked Gautier cautiously, 'Do you know Princes Street railway station, sir?'

'Yes. I passed it on my way here.'

'Could you meet me there later this morning? Shall we say at noon? I will wait for you in the ticket hall.'

'Did I understand you to say that you are a friend of Miss Macnab, sir?'

'I know her father and mother. She lives with them in Paris.'

Gautier had met the bank clerk in the railway station and they were walking together in the gardens below Princes Street. The clerk, whose name was Archie McFee was in a hurry to return to the bank, since he had only a break of half an hour for his lunch. Gautier had formed the impression that he was a typical Scot: hard-working, honest, brought up no doubt in the strict principles of the Presbyterian Church, but kind at heart.

'Maybe I should no be telling you this, sir, but it is obvious to me that Miss Macnab is in trouble. The lassie needs a friend.'

'What makes you think that?'

'Why else should she be wishing to sell her jewellery, and she the daughter of a diplomat?'

51

McFee explained that only the previous day Fiona Macnab had come into the bank and asked for his advice. Her funds were running short, she had said, and she wished to raise some money by selling some of her jewellery. Yet it had only been a day or two ago that she had changed a considerable sum of French francs into Scottish pounds.

'How could she have spent that money, well into four figures it was, in so short a time?'

'What did you say to her?'

'I suggested that she should best go to a pawnbroker or, failing that, to try one of the jewellers in the city.'

'Do you think she took your advice?'

'One canna tell. The poor lassie was distraught. That is why I decided to mention this to you, sir. She is clearly in distress and I thought that as a friend, you might be willing to help her.'

'You were right to do so, Mr McFee. Thank you.' Gautier asked him one more question 'Was there a gentleman with her when she visited your bank?'

'The first time there was; a foreign looking gentleman. The second time she came alone.'

They parted some distance from McFee's bank, as he did not wish to be seen returning from his lunch with a customer. Gautier knew that what he had heard left him no choice. He would have to speak to Fiona Macnab and find out how he could help her. If that meant she would find out that he was from the Sûreté and had been sent by her father, it could not be avoided.

He rang the bell at the Killiecrankie Hotel and when a maid came to the door he told her he had had called to see Fiona Macnab. The girl's expression changed immediately when he said the name and he could detect in it a suppressed excitement of the type often triggered off by a minor sensation or scandal. The maid told him that Miss Macnab was out and she could not say when she would return to the hotel. Gautier left, telling her he would call again, but did not give the girl his name. He had no wish to frighten Miss Macnab into leaving Edinburgh.

In London, as soon as Sylvie Lambert had given him the name of the hotel in Edinburgh where he would be staying, he had telegraphed Sûreté headquarters asking what progress had been made in the murder case he was handling. Ingrid was still on his conscience, so now he returned to the hotel and found that there was a telegram for him from Surat. It read: All the journalists in Rue Réamur have been placed under police surveillance by order of the Director General.

What depressed Gautier was learning that Courtrand had decided to interfere in the investigation. Theoretically he supposed all those who worked with Ingrid should be regarded as possible suspects in her murder, but he would have wanted some evidence of their involvement before putting them under police watch. He found a post office and tried to make a telephone call to Paris without success. Telephone operators in Scotland, he discovered, were just as autocratic as those in France and to frustrate him they made the excuse that they could not understand his accented English.

Evening was approaching so he returned to the environs of the Killiecrankie Hotel and, judging it was still too early to be sure of finding Fiona Macnab in the hotel, he went into the bar which he had visited the previous evening. There was always a chance, he supposed, that he might overhear some gossip about the girl's financial difficulties. After all one of the men he had sat next to in the bar had been a banker. In any case he had had no lunch and could fortify himself until he dined with another malt whisky.

He asked the barman if he could recommend a malt whisky from one of the islands of Scotland. Those who knew their whiskies, he had been told, believed that whisky distilled in the isles had a distinctive flavour of its own.

'I'll no give you an Islay whisky,' the barman said, 'for they're no to everyone's taste. Try this one from the Orkneys.'

Another aspect of drinking in Scotland which Gautier found odd was that one was obliged to pay for a drink as soon as it was served. In any French bistro or bar, however humble, one would only settle the bill as one was leaving. Did that mean that the Scots, and for that matter the English, were not to be trusted? He could not complain though about the Orkney whisky he had been given, finding in it an unusual richness and a lingering aftertaste which might well bring to mind the sturdy character of those who lived in northern climes.

As it happened he was glad that he had paid for his drink in advance, for from where he was sitting he could see through the front windows of the bar, and he had only taken a sip or two of the whisky when he saw Fiona Macnab passing outside in the street. She was walking slowly which was why he had been able to recognize her even in the fading light. Not waiting to finish his drink, he hurried out into the street and stopped her.

'Mademoiselle Macnab, is it not?' He asked her in French. She turned to face him.

'Do I know you, Monsieur?'

'We have met in Paris.' She hesitated so he went on. 'but you may not remember me.'

She still hesitated. Gautier sensed that her hesitation as well as the speed at which she had been walking might be a sign that she was reluctant to return to her hotel. If that were the case, he might turn it to his advantage. 'May I walk with you?' he asked.

'I am only going as far as my hotel which is just along the street,' she replied.

'In that case could we go somewhere else and talk?'

'Monsieur, I still do not remember who you are.'

Again she had hesitated before replying, so Gautier pressed on. 'Perhaps if you have no other engagement this evening, we might dine together.' He smiled the boyish, friendly smile which he had often used to disarm a woman. 'Surely there must be somewhere in this northern desolation where civilization prevails.'

In spite of herself Fiona Macnab smiled. 'You are too hard on the Scots, Monsieur.'

'Then you do know somewhere one can dine?'

There was a long pause before she capitulated. Reluctantly she admitted, 'I do know of a restaurant not far from here. In fact I was thinking of going there myself this evening.'

'Then you allow me to accompany you?'

'Well, if you insist. . . .'

They found a hansom cab at the end of the street and as they were being driven to the restaurant Gautier wondered how long it had been since she had eaten a full meal. Hunger could be a more powerful motive than social conventions. Some of the tension he had felt in her seemed to evaporate as soon as they were in the cab. Evidently she did not remember the name of the restaurant and she had to give the cabbie instructions as they journeyed, which thankfully did not give them time for conversation. On the way he looked at her. The remark Sir Donald had made about her not being a romantic schoolgirl, seemed to imply that she was plain. She was by no means beautiful, it was true, but one could see that had she taken more trouble with her appearance she would not be unattractive.

The restaurant was at one end of Princes Street not far from North Bridge. In its decor and ambience it was not unlike one of the larger Paris restaurants and Gautier decided that perhaps some of the traditions of the Auld Alliance lingered after all. Although he would have thought it early to be dining, the place was filling up, but they were given a table and as they were study-ing the menu he felt that Fiona was looking at him. He quickly called a waiter over to their table. Once they had ordered it would be more difficult for her to get up and leave.

Eventually she said, 'I do remember you now. You're Inspector Gautier, are you not?' He admitted he was and he could see indig-nation rising in her cheeks. 'So you have come to arrest me?' She had raised her voice and he was glad they were speaking in French.

'Mademoiselle, there can be no question of arresting you. In any case I do not have the authority to do so.'

'Then why are you here? My father sent you, did he not?'

'I am simply here to make sure that you are safe and well.'

'As you can see I am. Is that all you want?'

'And the companion with whom you travelled here from Paris?'

'He is no longer with me.'

'What will you do now? I understand your family has friends in Edinburgh.'

She looked down at her lap, so he would not be able to see the tears in her eyes. 'In the end I suppose I shall have to face the humiliation of asking them for help.'

'You need not do that. I can help you.'

She said nothing. A waiter brought them the soup they had ordered. The strange name of it, Cullen Skink, meant nothing to Gautier, but Fiona appeared to know it was a fish and potato soup and he had simply repeated her order. He was glad to see that the emotion she was feeling did not stop her eating. In the meantime he must decide how he could bring matters to a head and cruel though it might be, the easiest way might be to tell her how much he knew.

'You were not able to sell your jewellery then?'

Now the tears could not be halted. They ran down her cheeks as she tried to staunch their flowing with a handkerchief. 'I tried to sell the brooch my mother gave me on my twenty-first birthday, but they offered me such a derisory sum that I could not part with it.'

'Let us get down to practicalities. How much do you owe?'

'Only my hotel bill,' she replied and then blushed as she added, 'our bill.'

Gautier knew he must be ruthless. 'So he took all the money you changed at the bank? Where is he now?'

Fiona shrugged. 'I do not know for certain, but I have reason to believe he has gone to Ireland.'

They ate in silence for a time. Gautier wanted her to think, to face up to her situation, to recognize how few options remained to her. No doubt the friends in Edinburgh would take her in, but for how long could she stay with them? And would they be sympathetic when they knew the facts? Could she stay on in Scotland, find employment, be independent? For a girl with her sheltered background and few qualifications it would be difficult.

When he judged that she was ready, he suggested, 'Why not come back to Paris with me?'

'Never!'

'That is all your parents want. Can you not imagine how relieved they would be to have you back, how relieved and how delighted?'

'Oh yes? And is that why they put the police on to me? Treated me like a common criminal?'

Slowly, point by point he argued with her and slowly, grudgingly she retreated. They had finished their meal and were lingering over the last glass of wine when Gautier knew she had accepted defeat. She asked him, 'And how am I to travel? How can I pay the fare?'

'We will travel together.'

57

Looking down at Dover harbour from the rail of the cross-channel steamer, Gautier watched the preparations that were being
made for its departure. Early that morning he had settled his bill
at the hotel in Morningside, gone to the Killiecrankie Hotel,
where he had paid what Fiona Macnab owed and they had gone
together with their luggage and caught a train for London. He
might of course have given her money with which to settle her bill
the previous evening after their dinner, but he had not been
entirely certain that she would not have used it to go in pursuit of
her lover. He had no wish to follow her to Ireland.

From London they had travelled together by train to Dover and
booked passages on the night boat to Calais. He had been fortunate enough to find that there was one cabin available and Fiona
was now in it, asleep no doubt and preparing to meet her parents
in Paris. Before boarding the steamer in Dover, he had sent a
telegram to Sir Donald, telling him that his daughter would be
arriving at the Gare du Nord the following morning. He had
risked offending Sir Donald by adding at the end of the telegram
the words, 'A specially affectionate welcome would be appreciated'. Sir Donald had not struck him as demonstrative man.

He had also sent another telegram to Sylvie Lambert at the
French Embassy, explaining that he had been obliged to return to
Paris directly and therefore not able to take her out to dinner in
London as he had promised. That was a matter for regret as he
had enjoyed Sylvie's company, and he had added at the end of the
telegram that he hoped he would see her again before too long in
France if not in London. On the other hand he was glad to be
returning to Paris where he would be able to devote himself to
finding the man who had murdered Ingrid.

When at last the ship sailed light rain began to fall. Out at sea he realized that with rain, a freshening east wind and the darkness, it would be absurd to remain on deck, so he went below to the lounge in which passengers without cabins could wait until the voyage was completed. Many of them were there already, huddled up on the benches, some dozing, others being sick. Gautier had always found it surprising that as soon as a ship began moving slowly, without any discernible rolling or pitching, there would always be people who could not help being sick.

He and Fiona had been given a double cabin with two bunks and when he had installed her in it on her own, saying he would spend the night on deck, she had protested, saying she could see no reason why they could not share it. For a spinster and a Scot she seemed to be surprisingly broadminded. Now he went down to the cabin partly to reassure himself that she was all right and partly to escape the fetid atmosphere of the passenger lounge.

The cabin was in darkness except for a shaft of light that came into it under the door from outside, but he could make out her body, covered with a single blanket and stretched out on one of the bunks. She appeared to be sleeping soundly, so he thought it could do no harm if he were to sit on the other bunk and rest. It had been a long day. He sat there for a time and then, as Fiona still seemed to be sleeping, lay back and stretched out.

He must have fallen asleep and woke with a start to find someone lying alongside him. It was Fiona and she laughed as she said, 'I told you we could share the cabin'. She snuggled up to him and he became aware that she was naked. 'Make love to me,' she whispered.

'Is this a joke?' Gautier could not understand what she was doing. He had shown no sign of being attracted by her or of any sexual interest in her. Fiona did not reply but reached up with her arms, drew his face to hers and began covering it with urgent, inexpert kisses. She took his hand and lifted it to her breasts and her own hands slid down over his stomach. He tried to push her away but she was insistent and she was strong. Gautier became aware of the appeal of her naked body. Her breasts were fuller than one might have expected, her hips slim, her belly smooth. At any other time he might easily have given in to temptation, but he was conscious of his responsibilities. In a way it might be argued that he was on duty. He sat up and pushed her away, gently but firmly.

'Please Fiona, go back to your bunk.'

'How can you be so cruel? I have been treated like a naughty child, degraded. Am I to get nothing out of this humiliating escapade? Can you not give me a little comfort?'

'I am sorry, no.'

'Am I so repulsive?' She sat up and looked at him. 'Even Walther whom I brought to Scotland could not bear to have me in his bed.'

'You must not think like that. It is not that I do not find you attractive, but I have an obligation to your father.'

'*Merde* to you and *merde* to my father!'

She returned to the other bunk and he could hear her sobbing as she lay there; odd, pitiful noises like those of a small, wounded animal. Gautier waited and after a long time the noises stopped. Deciding that she was asleep, he left the cabin and returned to the discomfort and stench of the passenger lounge.

The train journey from Calais to Paris was tedious, seeming longer than usual. Throughout it Fiona hardly spoke and Gautier supposed she must be sulking. Only when they were on the outskirts of Paris did a little vitality seem to return to her, perhaps because she felt she would need her strength to face her parents. As the train was slowing down she stood up and faced him.

'My behaviour on the boat last night was inexcusable,' she said,

60

and to his surprise kissed him gently on the cheek. 'I apologize.'

Gautier smiled. 'Mademoiselle, you may find this difficult to believe, but in spite of all our differences, I have enjoyed the days we spent together.'

'Liar!' she said, but she was smiling.

Sir Donald Macnab and his wife were waiting on the platform and when she saw her daughter alighting from the train, Lady Macnab rushed up and threw her arms around her. Gautier could not hear what she said, but there tears on the cheeks of both women. Sir Donald stood watching them, but one could see the Adam's apple in his throat moving agitatedly, a sure sign of emotion in even the most phlegmatic of Scots.

He moved across to Gautier and shook his hand. 'Inspector, we owe you a debt of gratitude which we can never repay. I look forward to hearing your report later, but we have our daughter back and for the moment that is all that matters.'

The four of them left the station to where an automobile and chauffeur were waiting in the forecourt. Gautier watched as the family embarked and noticed that Fiona did not even look in his direction. He could understand why and even why Sir Donald's debt of gratitude did not extend to inviting him to join them in the auto as they were driven back into the centre of Paris.

5

A fiacre took Gautier to Place du Châtelet, where he stopped at a café for his breakfast. Around him scores of Parisians were doing the same thing, some hastily in case they might be late for work in the neighbouring offices and shops. He himself drank his coffee and ate his croissant slowly, wishing to recapture the comfortable feel of France again after the rigours of Scotland and the channel. On reflection he was glad that he had declined the offer of sex which Fiona had made to him on the cross-channel steamer, if for no other reason than that it would have felt like an affront to Ingrid.

He thought it unlikely that any progress would have been made in finding out who had killed her. A key factor in explaining any murder was understanding the motive behind it. Killings by paid assassins were common in Paris. One could have a person killed for as little as fifty francs, but even in these there was a motive, in fact one might say there were two; greed on the part of the killer and revenge, jealousy or again greed by the person who paid him. He was confident that no one would have paid to have Ingrid killed and yet someone must have had a motive for wishing her dead, although neither he nor anyone else who knew her would be able to suggest one. She was independent, worked on her own, had no rivals in her profession and, as far as Gautier knew, no lovers other than himself. The motive for her murder must be complex, perhaps political, and it was on this which he must concentrate now he was back in Paris.

After his breakfast, when he reached Sûreté headquarters the Director General had not arrived. Courtrand worked hours that even a gentleman might envy. So he left a message with his secretary Corbin, saying simply that he had completed the assignment he had been given, went to his own office and sent for Surat.

'I assume the journalists are still under police surveillance,' he said to him.

'As far as I know, *patron*, but I suspect that the surveillance is not too rigorous.'

Gautier made no comment. 'Have there been any new developments?'

'None. Her apartment has been searched again and all her papers and possessions examined, but they told us nothing. Madame's aunt came to Paris from Rotterdam and arranged for her body to be taken to Holland for the funeral.'

'I trust that she was treated with consideration and respect.'

Gautier's remark appeared to embarrass Surat. 'The old lady spent the night in Paris as she could not do the journey here and back in a day. I took her out to dinner, *patron*.'

Now Gautier understood his embarrassment. Looking after Ingrid's aunt should have been the responsibility of a senior officer and he knew Surat would only have acted if no one else had. Later he would find a way of repaying him what he had spent, but that could wait. First he must outline the plan he had formed for investigating Ingrid's murder. Journalists by what they wrote could often cause offence and domestic or even financial trouble. Besides the German paper for which she was the Paris correspondent, Ingrid had written a political column for *Le Gaulois* and occasional features for newspapers in Austria, Spain and Italy. More recently she

had contributed articles to the *Washington Post* from Brazil as well
as Paris. Gautier's plan was to study all the reports, articles and features she had written during the last month. If none of them suggested any possible reason for her murder, the search could be
extended back to two months, but the work involved would be considerable, for Ingrid wrote for many newspapers and magazines in
a number of countries. The assistance of translators would also be
needed since she had written in several languages. Some journalists,
Gautier knew, kept files of all the pieces they wrote, but he could
not remember seeing one, either in Ingrid's apartment or in her
desk at Rue Réamur. He told Surat to look for any such file and if
one could not be found they would have to trawl through the back
numbers of all the papers for which she had written.

'It may well be a long, tedious task, for Mademoiselle Van de
Velde was a prolific author,' he told Surat. 'We will tackle it together. But first check to see if you can find a master file anywhere.'

No sooner had Surat left when a messenger arrived to say that
the Director General wished to see the Chief Inspector as a matter of urgency. Courtrand was in his office, obviously still troubled by his liver, and impatient.

'So you are back already, Gautier,' he complained. 'Why did
you not come to see me sooner? And as you are back what do you
have to report?'

'Mademoiselle Macnab is safe and back with her family,
Monsieur.'

'And the man who abducted her?'

'As far as I know he is in Ireland, Monsieur.'

Gautier told Courtrand how he had found Fiona Macnab
stranded and penniless in Edinburgh, how he had brought her
back to Paris and how she had been united with her parents at the
Gare du Nord that morning. Courtrand listened without showing
any signs of approval or even satisfaction.

'You should have informed that you were returning.' he complained, 'and I could have joined the ambassador and his wife at the station to greet his daughter.'

'Sir Donald asked me if I could tell him later what had happened in England. Why not go round to the British Embassy later this morning and give him a full report, Monsieur?'

'A good idea, Gautier. After all the report should come from me.' Courtrand's mood brightened. 'I will go at noon. Then he can scarcely not offer me lunch in the embassy.'

At about the time when Courtrand was being driven to the British Embassy, Gautier was walking along Boulevard St Germain, heading for the Café Corneille. The café was one of hundreds in Paris where men went to take an aperitif or a glass of wine before their midday meal. Many of them tended to attract men working in a particular trade and one could find cafés for almost every *métier*: for actors, printers, jewellers, tailors and even moneylenders.

The Café Corneille did not fall into any one such category and its habitués were drawn from a catholic selection of occupations including the law, journalism and publishing. In most cafés police officers were not welcome. The reason for this was that during times of political unrest and particularly during the wave of anarchism which had swept the country a few years previously, police had sometimes been sent to mingle with people in cafés either to identify troublemakers or to act as agents provocateurs. Gautier was secretly proud of the fact that he had been accepted in the small circle of friends who met regularly at the Café Corneille. Tactfully and out of respect for him they never discussed or even mentioned any crime or other matter which might be the subject of police investigation when he was present, but in all other respects he was treated like any other members of their coterie.

When he arrived at the café that morning only three of his

usual group were there: Duthrey, a journalist who worked for *Le Figaro* and a close friend of his, Froissart, who owned a bookshop on the Left Bank, and an elderly judge. As often happened they were discussing the current political situation. Everyone knew that a war with Germany was inevitable, if only to satisfy the national pride of the French, still wounded after the humiliating defeat of 1871. The political manoeuvring which was then taking place in Europe was aimed at ensuring that when it came, France had allies she could trust. One reliable ally, Great Britain, had been secured in 1904 by the signing of the Entente Cordiale. Russia was potentially another, but confidence in her had quickly evaporated only a year later after her defeat by Japan, followed by an abortive attempt at a working class revolution in St Petersburg.

'The British are not to be trusted,' Froissart was saying. 'Their first priority is to develop their colonial empire, not to safeguard the interests of France.'

The judge agreed. 'They see their empire as an outlet for goods from their growing industries.'

'We must not allow them to infiltrate North Africa at any cost,' Duthrey said. 'The protection and development of the peoples of North Africa are France's responsibility.'

'If we take that attitude,' Gautier commented, 'we may even lose the support of Britain.'

'In diplomacy perhaps, but never in a war,' the judge said. 'The British will be driven into any war by their armament manufacturers.'

He was referring obliquely to the policy followed by major British manufacturers of guns and all the accoutrements of war. One company had even installed its representative in Paris, providing him with a lavish income and a well-staffed house, from which he was able to penetrate the top social and political circles and so to have an influence on the decisions of the French government. Not long ago as Gautier knew, this representative had played a significant part in a major crime, but not one for which he could be indicted.

As they were talking two more of their regular group arrived. One was a young lawyer whose practice was thriving largely on the strength of the work he was doing on divorces, which until recently had been virtually impossible to obtain, but were now becoming fashionable. The other arrival was a member of the National Assembly, the deputy for Seine-et-Marne. The deputy always enlivened discussions at the Café Corneille, by throwing out seemingly at random rumours about current matters of state, which frequently proved to be groundless.

When he heard what the other members of their group were discussing he remarked, 'Are you saying that the war with Germany will erupt over North Africa? You are wrong. The trouble will start in the Balkans.'

'What makes you believe that?' the judge asked.

'Germany is obliged to tolerate and even encourage the aspirations that Austro-Hungary has in the Balkans, just to make sure of keeping her in their alliance. It is a dangerous policy. The Habsburg Empire has left Europe with a legacy of trouble in the Balkans which only war will resolve.'

'You are right,' Froissart agreed. 'Having two such different countries under a single monarchy is a recipe for disaster.'

His statement triggered off an argument. Members of their group in the Café Corneille were all articulate and took a lively interest in politics, but their arguments were conducted with good humour. Some of them were well disposed towards Austria, even though they were agreed that trouble was to be expected in the Balkans. The discussion was continuing when another journalist member arrived to join them. Mathieu was on the staff of *Mercure de France*, a literary review first published by a group of writers less than twenty years previously. Although the review concentrated mainly on the works of leading authors in France, Mathieu seemed to have contacts in many parts of Europe and through them was always well informed on political matters.

After listening to what the others in the group were saying, he remarked, 'I agree with you in principle about the Balkans, but we should not rule out the possibility that the next war might start in Austria. There are signs of trouble in Vienna already.'

'What signs?'

'I heard only this morning that a good friend of mine, a journalist named Igor Andrassy, who contributed to our review from time to time has been assassinated. There seems little doubt that the murder was for political motives.'

Andrassy, Gautier remembered, was the name of the journalist whom Philippe Crespelle had said was friendly with Ingrid when they were living in Vienna. He made no comment and was glad that the others in the café did not pursue the matter of Andrassy's murder. There were other ways by which he could find out whether it might be connected with that of Ingrid. In any case the others in their group soon grew tired of talking about the politics of the Austro-Hungarian Empire and of speculating on the likelihood of a European war. The conversation switched to matters nearer home and to the recent behaviour of the President of France.

After their experience with kings and emperors, the French wanted a Republic, but they never tired of mocking the men who were given the office of President. The gaffes of Macmahon, the efforts of Grévy to conceal the corruption of his son-in-law and more recently the revelation that Félix Faure had died in the Elysée Palace clutching the hair of his naked mistress, had delighted the *boulevardiers* of Paris as well as the patrons of the cafés.

Only later, when he and Duthrey had left the Café Corneille and were walking along Boulevard St Germain, did Gautier refer to what Mathieu had told them. 'Did you by any chance know this Igor Andrassy who was murdered in Vienna?' he asked.

'Only by reputation,' Duthrey replied. 'He was respected as thoroughly professional and a worthy colleague.'

Gautier felt that he should explain why he had asked the question. 'I am told that when she was living in Vienna, Ingrid Van de Velde worked closely with Andrassy.'

'*Mon vieux*, I was devastated when I heard about Madame Van de Velde.' It was the first time that the two men had met since Ingrid's murder. He touched Gautier on the arm. 'You have my most profound sympathy,'

At the next street corner Duthrey found a fiacre which would drive him home to the excellent lunch which his wife would have waiting for him. Gautier was not sorry to see him leave, for he had no wish to hear more of his condolences about Ingrid, however sympathetic, nor to answer any questions about her death. As he walked on and crossed the Seine on his way to Place Dauphine where he would take his own lunch, he found himself wondering guiltily whether this reluctance might be an indication that the grief he had felt was already diminishing.

Back in his office at the Sûreté that afternoon Gautier began making a list of all the newspapers for whom Ingrid had been a regular correspondent, or to whom she made occasional contributions.

His list was based on the curriculum vitae he had found in her writing bureau for he wished to see all the articles she had written during the past month. This should present no problem as far as the *Leipziger Volkszeitung*, *Le Gaulois* and the *Washington Post* were concerned, since all these papers would keep back issues on file and would be glad to supply copies of what she had written to the police. In the case of lesser-known publications research might be needed. Before he had finished making his list, Surat arrived in his office, carrying what looked like a bundle of crumpled paper tied together with string.

'What do you have there?' Gautier asked him.

'Rubbish, *patron*, but it may save us a great deal of work.'

He had found the papers, he explained to Gautier, in a bin full of rubbish on the floor of the building immediately below Ingrid's apartment. As he had already told Gautier the concierge was inclined to neglect her duties, particularly when she had been drinking on the previous evening. Among the rubbish he had found what could only be articles which Ingrid had written together with a small number of letters. He had reasoned that whoever had killed Ingrid must have suspected that there might be something in the articles which could suggest that he might have murdered her. So rather than leave the building carrying armfuls of paper, he had thrown them all into the first rubbish bin he could find, assuming that the concierge would empty it the following morning.

'A clever piece of deduction,' Gautier commented, 'and I have no doubt that you are right. Let us get down to work.'

Together they began sorting the articles, separating them according to the journals for which they had been written. Checking the articles written in French presented no problem and Gautier's command of English was sufficient for the few that had been written in English. Those in German or Dutch could be sent downstairs to the small department of the Sûreté which provided translation services whenever they were required. Those in any of the Balkan languages would have to be sent outside, probably to one of the faculties of the Sorbonne.

As Gautier knew, Ingrid had been a prolific writer and knowledgeable, with an interest in a wide range of subjects and disciplines, which was the reason why she had been so successful as a journalist. Checking all the articles she had written took him and Surat the best part of the afternoon, and in none of them they could find anything which even hinted at any possible reason for her murder. Only one, a letter in German written in a sprawling hand, caught Gautier's interest. The letter was no more than a note and was signed with an indecipherable single word.

He handed the letter to Surat. 'Take this letter to our linguists downstairs,' he said, and ask them if they can give us at least an indication of what it says. I am not looking for a verbatim translation, just a summary. It is very short.'

While Surat was away, Gautier forgot about the articles and thought instead of Walther Kossuth, the man with whom Fiona Macnab had travelled to Scotland and who had abandoned her. Sylvie Lambert had said he was Hungarian and an agitator. Sir Donald Macnab had described him as a plausible rogue and had said that he had seen Fiona dancing with the man at a ball, which suggested that he must have had contacts in Paris society. On the other hand he had stolen what money Fiona had taken with them to Scotland, presumably so that he could get away to Ireland.

There would be ways of finding out how long Kossuth had been in Paris and what he had been doing. Gautier thought it unlikely that he had entered Paris illegally, for he had a passport even though it might be a false one. In fact one of his motives for travelling with Fiona, apart from using her money, might have been that he would have less difficulty in entering England with a dubious passport if he were accompanying a woman who had diplomatic immunity. He would also have lodged somewhere in Paris, probably not in one of the better hotels since he must have been short of money. When they had finished their scrutiny of Ingrid's articles, he would tell Surat to arrange for policemen to visit the lesser-known hotels to see whether they had any record of a Kossuth having stayed there. The work would be slow and time consuming, but for the present he had no other leads to follow. That did not depress him, for solving a murder always required patience.

When Surat returned he was carrying the handwritten note and another single sheet of paper. He handed the sheet to Gautier. 'Translating the note,' he said, 'took less time than making out the signature of the person who wrote it.'

The note read: 'I have two pieces of news from the Balkans. One is that Kossuth has been in Paris for some time. The other is that I have learnt the identity of BB. Sorry we did not have time to discuss this today but perhaps we can have a word when I return to Paris'.

Not until next morning was it possible to learn a little more about Andrassy. The Ministry for Foreign Affairs had been able to say that he had been invited to the meeting where he had been seen speaking to Ingrid, as the representative of the Austrian newspaper *Kleine Zeitung*. Andrassy had not been on the permanent staff of that or any other paper, but like Ingrid he had contributed to a number of them in other countries as well as in Austria and was known to visit Paris often. On the surface he appeared to be a reputable journalist and Gautier could see no reason for doubting his integrity. Duthrey had spoken highly of him. It was true that Philippe Crespelle had hinted that the British Embassy in Vienna had been concerned about his activities to the extent of having him watched, but in Gautier's experience diplomats could be paranoid in their suspicions, especially about journalists.

The Ministry for Foreign Affairs had been able to give an address where Andrassy could be contacted when he was in Paris. It was a small but respectable hotel on the Left Bank, not too far from the Chambre des Députés and therefore well placed for any visitor with an interest in politics. Surat was already on his way there to find out if the management could tell him anything about the movements of Andrassy during his last visit to Paris. In the meantime Gautier had telegraphed an official request to the police in Vienna for information about the murder of Andrassy, giving the reason that it might be connected with a murder in Paris.

He wondered whether he should call again at the office from which Ingrid had worked and then decided against it. Neuhoff had evidently seen Andrassy talking to Ingrid, but had not even known his name and it seemed unlikely therefore that the other journalists in the office would either. Kossuth appeared to be the only link between Ingrid and Andrassy and one could not rule out the possibility that Kossuth had murdered Ingrid, which might explain why he had left Paris, very probably in a hurry. Gautier knew now at least that if Ingrid had been killed by a lover whom she had taken back to her apartment, that lover could not have been Andrassy.

6

The following morning when Gautier arrived at the British Embassy residence the door was opened to him not by a housemaid, but by a manservant wearing a morning coat. When he asked whether Miss Fiona Macnab was at home, the man said he would find out and took the card which Gautier held out to him. Gautier always carried two cards, one with his official position at the Sûreté, the other printed simply with his name and private address. This time he used the personal card, not because he thought it would make Fiona more inclined to see him, but to suggest that although he had come on official business, the business was not so grave that she would need to have her mother or an embassy official to chaperone her. He had formed the impression that she was a young woman whose impulses had too often been restrained by the conventions of society, and he thought he would learn more from her if they were alone when they talked.

Another reason for informality was that he had decided to call on her without telling the Director General. Courtrand took little interest in the day-to-day workings of crime detection, but he was obsessed by the grandeur of diplomacy and in particular by Franco-British relations. He would have expected to be informed of Gautier's plan to speak with the British Ambassador's daughter and might well have insisted on accompanying him.

Presently the manservant returned and led him to a small room where Fiona was waiting. She was fashionably dressed but wore a hat which indicated that she had been on the point of leaving the house. That should not have surprised him since she was not French. French ladies of society hardly ever left home in the mornings, except perhaps to take a ride in the Bois de Boulogne, or to leave visiting cards at the homes of their friends. Indeed there were no other reasons for a lady to leave home. Couturiers, dressmakers, milliners and hairdressers would all call at the house to meet her requirements.

Fiona held out a gloved hand to be kissed, saying, 'Inspector, I did not expect to be seeing you again so soon. You have not come to arrest me, I trust.'

Gautier smiled. 'No, Mademoiselle, I have come to ask for your help.'

'Oh yes?'

He sat down opposite her in a chair that she pointed out to him. She was behaving like a gracious hostess, but with a measure of condescension. He sensed that any of the gratitude which she may have been trying to express on the train as it pulled into Paris the previous morning, had disappeared.

'We need to know how we can reach the gentleman who travelled with you to Scotland.'

'Why? I have no wish to press charges against him,' Fiona said sharply.

'This has nothing to do with his behaviour in Scotland. We wish to interview him on an entirely different matter.'

'You must think me a fool, Inspector. My father has put you up to this.'

'I assure you, Mademoiselle, your father knows nothing of this matter. We believe that Monsieur Kossuth may be able to help us in solving a crime that has been committed in Vienna.'

'He has not been in Vienna for months.'

'No one is saying that he committed the crime, but we believe he has information which might help us.'

Fiona looked at Gautier and he could see that she did not trust him. When she did speak it was clear that she had decided to take shelter in indignation. 'What sort of person do you think I am? Walther and I may have had our differences, but do you really imagine that I would betray him to the police?'

Gautier tried to tell her it was not a question of betrayal, but she would not listen. As her indignation rose so did her voice. Was this the way that the police always behaved, she demanded, playing people against each other, trying to subvert their loyalties, tricking them into confessions? She refused to be treated like some common police informer; she would tell him nothing. If he pestered her again she would report him to the Prefect of Police.

Realizing that they had reached an impasse, Gautier left. He had not really expected that a woman's pride would have allowed her to speak against the man who had abandoned her, and in any case she seemed to know little about Kossuth. His principal reason for going to see Fiona that morning had been to keep at least a channel of communication open with her. He did not know why. Now if her treatment of him that morning had been a retaliation for the indignities she had suffered in Scotland, she might perversely be more amenable to any approaches he might make to her in the future.

When he arrived back at Sûreté headquarters he found that Surat had not returned from visiting the hotel where Andrassy had usually stayed when he was in Paris, nor had there been any reply to the telegram which he had sent to Vienna. What he really needed to know was why Andrassy had left Paris to return home. Some days had elapsed since Ingrid had been murdered and he had only heard of Andrassy's murder at the Café Corneille the previous day. Although in the note he had sent to Ingrid he had suggested a meeting, one could not know whether they had in fact met.

With no immediate plan in mind, he had begun reading once more through the articles Surat had found, when a messenger came up to tell him that a Monsieur Edgar Wright had arrived and was asking to see him. Although he had never met him, Gautier knew that Wright was an Englishman who several months previously had arrived in Paris to take up his duties as the new representative of the British armaments manufacturing company, Lydon-Walters. Wright's predecessor, a Greek named Valanis, had achieved notoriety, both by his lifestyle and his transparent attempts to influence French government policy. In the few months that he had been in Paris, Wright had been more discreet and less visible and Gautier could think of no reason why he should not see him, and told the messenger to bring him up to his office.

Although a small man, Wright proved to be good-looking and had the manner of a well-educated Englishman. Unlike most Englishmen, though, he spoke French fluently. After they had exchanged the usual courtesies he sat facing Gautier across his desk.

'I hope I will not be wasting your time, Inspector,' he said, 'but I felt it was my duty to come and see you.'

'Monsieur?'

'I have been told that the journalist Mademoiselle Van de Velde has been murdered. Is that true?'

'I regret to say, Monsieur Wright, that it is.'

'Well, I ought to tell you that recently she came to interview me. From what I have heard it must have been on the very day that she was killed.'

'At what time of the day was this?'

'In the afternoon.'

'Are you certain of that?'

Wright appeared to be almost offended by the question. Gautier supposed he must at least have heard of the time when Ingrid had been murdered. He also wondered whether Wright must know of his relations with her, which was why he had come to see him. Then he told himself that now he was being paranoid.

'Perfectly,' he said firmly. 'She came to my home. The servants will be able to confirm that.'

'May I ask you why she came to see you, Monsieur?'

'To interview me, but I believe there may have been an element of deception in the request.'

'In what way?'

Wright explained that when Ingrid had asked if she might interview him, she had given the impression that she wished to write a piece about him as a new figure in Paris society. Articles of that type, on 'personalities' in the social scene, were appearing more and more frequently in the leading newspapers. When she had gone to see him however, the questions she had asked him had not been about him or his career or his family, but about the company which he represented. She claimed to have heard that Lydon-Walters had developed a revolutionary type of field gun which would give any army possessing it an enormous advantage in war.

'As we talked,' Wright said, 'her questions took on a decidedly political slant. She had evidently learned that our company had representatives in a number of European capitals as well as Paris; Berlin, for example, and Brussels and St Petersburg.'

'And Vienna?'

Wright smiled, although it did not seem that he had welcomed the question. 'Yes, and Vienna. Mademoiselle Van de Velde was not only well informed, but a very perceptive young lady.'

'Like many people,' Gautier said, 'she was probably trying to assess whether there might be any impending changes in the political balance of Europe.'

'A popular field for speculation,' Wright remarked. Then after a moment's hesitation, he asked, 'Do you know whether Mademoiselle Van de Velde actually wrote anything based on her interview with me? I could find nothing in the next day's *Le Gaulois*, and she would hardly have had time to send anything to the *Leipziger Volkszeitung*.'

Wright's question annoyed Gautier. The man had shown no concern over Ingrid's death, nor offered even a token expression of sympathy. He may well have a reason other than mere vanity for wishing to discover whether Ingrid had written about him or his company, but even if he did not know about Gautier's relationship with Ingrid, his callous enquiry had been inexcusable.

'I cannot say,' he replied and then he added: 'We know that Mademoiselle Van de Velde was working very closely with another journalist, a Magyar from Vienna named Igor Andrassy.'

He had tossed the remark into their conversation almost at random, curious to learn whether Wright might have heard of Andrassy. The effect it had was surprising.

Wright was clearly disconcerted and one could detect in his expression a hint of alarm, which he quickly concealed with a show of self-assurance.

'In that case, Inspector,' he replied, 'perhaps I should consult the *Kleine Zeitung*. Is that not the paper for which this Andrassy wrote?'

'You may find something there,' Gautier replied, 'although I should perhaps tell you that Andrassy too has been murdered.'

After Wright had left Gautier's irritation was slow in abating. He had been irritated when he realized that Wright's reason for coming to see him was not, as he claimed, to do his duty but to find out whether Ingrid had written anything about his company or himself. He was even more irritated by the man's indifference to the fact that she had been brutally murdered.

He knew it would be unwise to rule out the possibility that Wright might have been implicated in her murder, not personally for he did not have the style and probably not the courage of a killer, but he could use his company's wealth to manipulate people when it suited his purpose. Gautier had no illusions about the ruthless use of power by major companies. The alarm Wright had shown when Gautier had first mentioned Andrassy's name had bordered on panic when he was told of his murder, and it was clear that he must in some way be involved in the politics of the Balkans. That did not justify placing him under surveillance, but there were other ways of finding out more about him. Gautier had contacts in the government ministries which handled the procurement of arms, and a few enquires about Wright's past and the way he handled his company's business might be rewarding.

He was still deciding what action he should take in that direction, when Surat arrived back from his visit to Andrassy's hotel. He had little of any consequence to report. Andrassy had come to Paris at least once, and occasionally twice a month, always staying at the same hotel. Like most journalists he was not a secretive man, but he had never told any of the hotel's staff the purpose of his visits. He had from time to time taken a woman back to his room in the evenings, but by all accounts he had been a handsome, virile fellow, so that was only to be expected.

'One gets the impression,' Surat said, 'that his interests in life were cultural rather than political.'

'Very probably. He contributed to a French literary review.'

'Most of his visits to Paris came at the time of a cultural event

– the annual Salon, or the first night of a new drama by Sardou, even the publication of a new novel.'

Gautier was glad that Surat had not pursued the subject of Andrassy's love life when he was in Paris, or he might have discovered that it had included assignations with Ingrid. That thought was followed immediately by another. Perhaps he had found out that she had been Andrassy's lover and was too tactful to mention it. Gautier told himself that this was carrying suspicion to absurdity, but it was a depressing reminder that the memory of Ingrid still lingered in his mind.

He and Surat discussed Andrassy's movements during his last visit to Paris. Little was known about them, beyond the fact that he had spent one day visiting art exhibitions. A remark he had made to the hotel's proprietor appeared to confirm that he had intended to attend a meeting of the press, which must have been the same one at which her colleague Neuhoff had heard Ingrid talking to a man in a Balkan language. There was no means of knowing whether they had ever met on other occasions to discuss the mysterious BB. Andrassy's last visit to Paris had apparently been for only two days and had mainly been spent on visits to art galleries and other activites associated with cultural matters.

'I will return to the hotel and talk to junior members of the staff,' Surat said. 'They may know more about what this fellow was up to.'

After Surat had left, Gautier reflected on what he had to recognize had been an unsatisfactory morning's work. His meeting with Fiona Macnab had ended in acrimony, Edgar Wright's visit had been an irritation without telling him anything of value and he knew almost nothing about Andrassy which he had not known before.

His investigation into Ingrid's murder was making no progress and he was beginning to wonder whether it might be wiser for him to hand it over to another of the inspectors in the Sûreté. He did not believe that his relationship with Ingrid was in any way affecting his judgement, but memories of her continued to slip into his thoughts at inconvenient moments. They had been lovers it was true, but not in love, and they had never hinted at the possibility of making any closer arrangement. It was time he accepted that she was dead and, without ever forgetting her, continue with the daily business of living his life.

Before he had reached a decision a messenger came up from the ground floor bringing mail which had arrived for him at Sûreté headquarters. Among it was a reply to the telegram he had sent to the police in Vienna asking for information about Andrassy's murder. He could see that it was only a holding reply, telling him that a copy of the full report on the current situation in the case had been posted to him. The other item in the mail was an invitation. Elegantly printed on gilt-edged card, it invited Monsieur Jean-Paul Gautier to a soirée at the home of the Duchesse de Nièvre.

The *duchesse*, Gautier knew, held a special place in Paris life. For more than twenty years, as long as her husband the *duc* was alive, her presence had been essential to the success of any soirée, diner, ball or other social event in the upper echelons of Paris society. In a perverse way even those she declined to attend had acquired a certain distinction. The fact that even though beautiful and seductive she had refused to sleep with that distinguished womanizer the Prince of Wales, had only added to her lustre.

As she grew older, and without the reassuring bulwark of her husband, she had begun to have intellectual aspirations. Writers, poets and even musicians were invited to her home. Her other guests did not mind because she was rich enough to afford such eccentricities and her reputation remained above reproach. Even so Gautier could not understand why he had been honoured with an invitation. Then he remembered that not long ago she had written to the poet Verlaine inviting him to dine at her home even though he had been dead for more than ten years. Could it be that she thought that Gautier too had passed away? He smiled, wondering whether he should imitate the well-born but elderly bachelor who, finding that his name had slipped off the guests lists of all the leading hostesses, had angrily complained that reports of his death had been 'a gross exaggeration'.

Even though Gautier now realized that it was through no fault of his own, over the next two days the pace of the Sûreté's investigation into Ingrid's murder dwindled to almost nothing. He spent most of Sunday alone and brooding over his failure to have any sudden flash of inspiration. On Monday the report from Vienna on the death of Andrassy had arrived, but was disappointing. The facts were that he had been shot while walking through one of the public gardens in the centre of the city, on his way home to the apartment where he lived with his wife and two children. Two shots had been fired at him, with a revolver the police thought, one into his stomach and the second as he slumped forward into his throat. Both shots had been fired at very short range, suggesting that his assailant had been known to Andrassy. The revolver had not been found at the scene of the crime, nor had any other evidence which might point at the identity of the murderer. The rest of the report showed that in the opinion of the authorities in Vienna, Andrassy had been a law-abiding citizen with no reputation for violence, nor any criminal convictions. If there were any further developments in the case the Sûreté would be informed in case these had any bearing on the murder it was investigating.

Learning that Andrassy had left a wife and two children saddened Gautier. Now he dismissed any thought that he and Ingrid might ever have been lovers, either in Paris or Vienna. Although

Surat's enquiries had suggested that the man may well have enjoyed sexual adventures while he was away from home, Ingrid would never have condoned anything which might have damaged his family life. He went over all the ground he had covered once again, read the reports and the statements and even began checking all the articles which Surat had found. It was only on Monday afternoon that he remembered the invitation he had received, and that the soirée of the Duchesse de Niévre was to be held that evening. He had accepted the invitation even though it had arrived much later than convention would have demanded, deciding that once again he had been asked as a single man simply to make up the numbers. At soirées one might at the very least pick up useful information from an indiscreet remark.

The *duchesse* lived in a fine old house in the Faubourg Saint-Germain, that strip of land along the Left Bank which had escaped the ravages of Baron Haussmann when he had rebuilt the centre of Paris, and which was where the old aristocratic families had lived for generations. Even today, though some of them were migrating across the Seine to the avenues running down from Etoile to the Bois de Boulogne, the Faubourg remained the traditional home of 'Le Monde' or upper crust of Paris society.

When, after returning home to change into evening dress, Gautier arrived at the home of the *duchesse*, he was shown up to the drawing room where the guests were assembling. The *duchesse* received him at the entrance to the room where she was standing with the Comte de Fresnes, an elderly widower who had agreed to support her in hosting the evening. Gautier had never previously met the *comte* but he knew of his reputation. Though married to the pretty daughter of a rich banker, he had for many years been a dedicated sexual predator, pursuing women relentlessly until his wife had died of shame. Only one of his five children was still on speaking terms with him. The *duchesse* allowed

Gautier to kiss her hand but he had the impression that she had no idea who he was. The *comte* gave him a conspiratorial smile.

A young Polish pianist was to give a recital at the soirée and while waiting for him to perform, the guests were drinking champagne and exchanging gossip. Gautier could see few people among them whom he knew and he began to wonder whether he had been invited to the soirée by mistake. Then he saw the Prefect of Police. That was no cause for surprise. The Prefect was a social animal who found nothing more stimulating than to mix with the leaders of society. He was also popular and for that reason never short of invitations. When he saw Gautier in the room he beckoned him over to join him.

'Gautier, I did not expect to find you here,' he said.

'I was surprised to be invited, Monsieur le Préfet. Perhaps the *duchesse* mistook me for Verlaine.'

The Prefect laughed. 'I must tell the *duchesse* that. She has a good sense of humour, you know.'

Gautier was tempted to comment that in view of her frequent gaffes it was as well that the *duchesse* had a sense of humour, but he decided that the Prefect might disapprove, thinking the remark impertinent. He had always enjoyed an excellent relationship with the Prefect, who was known to think highly of his ability and had more than once defended him against Courtrand's malice.

'I have heard very flattering reports of you, Gautier,' the Prefect said. 'It seems you did the British Ambassador a great service.'

'It was an assignment I wish I had not been asked to undertake.'

'Nevertheless you did well to bring that unfortunate girl home, without fuss and without scandal.'

'I would call her unhappy rather than unfortunate.'

'Both. She is thirty and has never had a suitor. At one time there was talk of her marrying a Frenchmen, an aristocrat, but it came to nothing and the young man left the country.'

'What was his name?' Gautier asked.

'I am afraid I do not know. This happened some years ago before I became Prefect, but I understand the marriage fell through because the girl's father would not supply a dowry. The Scots do not believe in dowries apparently. The young man had been borrowing money on the expectations of the dowry and was placed in such financial difficulties that he had to leave the country. They say the poor girl was very upset about it. One might think that she still shows the scars.'

Gautier would have liked to have learnt more about Fiona's past. On the last occasion that he had seen her she had not tried to hide the bitterness she felt now, and the reasons for it might stretch back in time: the collapse of a prospective marriage; the way Kossuth had exploited and then abandoned her; the indignity of having the police sent to bring her back from Scotland; his rebuff of her sexual advances on the boat returning home. Yet he could not believe that discontent and resentment were part of her nature.

The Prefect though was not inclined to discuss Fiona and was more interested in the other guests at the soirée. 'I notice that Monsieur Edgar Wright, the representative of the British armaments firm has also been invited this evening,' he said, nodding in the direction of the doorway where the *duchesse* was standing. Gautier saw that Wright had just arrived and his name was called out by a footman as he moved forward to be received by his hostess. 'Have you met the man yet?'

'As a matter of fact I have. He came to see me in my office and asked me a number of questions.'

'About what?'

'The murder of the journalist, Mademoiselle Van de Velde.'

The reply clearly embarrassed the Prefect. 'The effrontery of the man!' he said. Then he added, 'I was so sorry to hear about

Ingrid. You must be devastated, Gautier. She was a good friend of yours, was she not?'

Gautier supposed he should not be surprised to learn that the Prefect knew about his relationship with Ingrid. The man had an uncanny knack of finding out all about the private lives of those who worked for him. Even so he was vaguely irritated that Ingrid's name should have been brought into their conversation. In his own way the Prefect was being tactful. At least he had used the expression 'good friend' and not the faintly condescending 'petite amie', although he must have known that their relationship had not been platonic.

At that point their conversation was halted, for the Comte de Fresnes went to the centre of the drawing room, held up his hand to silence the chatter and announced that the Polish pianist was ready to play. More chairs were brought into the room so that the ladies could sit as they listened to the music, while the men were to stand.

As they moved away towards the fringes of the room, the Prefect said, 'Come and see me tomorrow morning in my office, Gautier. There are things about Monsieur Wright which you should know.'

The Polish pianist was an energetic musician but not outstandingly talented. At least the recital gave Gautier an opportunity to see whom else among the guests he might know, and it was only then that he saw that Fiona Macnab was among them. One reason why he might not have noticed her before was that there seemed to be little to distinguish her from the other women in the room. Bright colours were the fashion that year and she was wearing a long pale green dress decorated with darker green leaves running down the full length of it. It may have been because of the green that he noticed for the first time that her hair had an auburn tinge to it. Red hair, he had heard, was a common feature of the Celtic people – Scots as well as Irish. He could not see her father or mother in the room and when the piano recital was over, as she appeared to be alone, he went over to her.

'Inspector Gautier!' Although she did not hold out her hand to be kissed, he seemed to sense that her mood was less abrasive than at their last meeting.

'Are your mother and father not here?' he asked her.

'No, my father has been recalled to London for consultation.'

Gautier smiled. 'Does that not usually mean a frostiness in diplomatic relations? What have we French done to upset the British this time?'

'You of all people should know the answer to that,' Fiona replied, but she was smiling. 'Anyway, my mother decided to go with him to London and buy some new outfits for herself.'

'Does she not shop for clothes in Paris?'

'No. She believes French fashions do not suit her.' Fiona paused and then she said, 'I am glad that you are here this evening, Jean-Paul, for I owe you an apology. When you called to see me the other day, I was unnecessarily stern with you.'

'No doubt I deserved it.'

'Not at all. You were so kind and considerate to me in Scotland and on the journey home. It was gratitude you deserved, not rudeness.'

Gautier smiled. 'It is always difficult to feel gratitude to one's jailers.'

Fiona laughed and seemed to reflect for a few moments. Then she said, 'That is a profound remark. It explains why I have never given my father and mother the gratitude they deserve. In a way I have always thought of them as jailers.'

'They are only concerned for your well-being and your happiness.'

Fiona reached out and laid a hand on his arm. 'And you and I? Can we forget my ingratitude and start again?'

Before he had time to answer, Gautier noticed that Edgar Wright was crossing the room towards them. He guessed immediately that Wright wished to speak to Fiona, although he did not know why.

'Inspector Gautier!' Wright called out even before he reached them. 'We meet again. I certainly did not expect to find you here.'

'My habit of appearing at times and places where I am not expected is one which some people find disconcerting,' Gautier replied.

'I can certainly agree with that,' Fiona remarked laughing.

Wright looked at her expectantly, obviously waiting to be introduced so Gautier obliged him. 'So you are the British Ambassador's daughter?' He held on to Fiona's hand longer than convention would demand. 'I am delighted to meet you, my dear.'

'You know my father? He is in England just now.'

'And you have not long returned from Edinburgh? Tell me, what did you think of Scotland. I know the country well.'

'Mine was a private visit,' Fiona replied brusquely.

'And what did your companion think of Scotland?'

Fiona blushed and Gautier could see that Wright's questions were annoying her, but he was not going to be easily diverted. He went on, 'So you must have come here this evening on your own?'

'I did, yes.'

'Then may I have the pleasure of escorting you home? Paris is not a city where single ladies can travel alone.'

Fiona had her reply ready. 'That is very kind of you, Monsieur, but Inspector Gautier has kindly agreed to see me home.'

'Ah well! Another time perhaps?'

Wright lingered with them for a little longer and then moved away, in no way disconcerted by Fiona's abruptness and still smiling. One could understand why he must be a successful salesman. After he had left, Fiona turned to Gautier.

'I hope you will not mind my using you as a protective shield, Inspector.'

'Not at all, Mademoiselle.'

'And will you then escort me home? What Monsieur Wright says is true. If people saw me leave here alone they would be shocked.'

Gautier hesitated but only briefly. 'It will be a pleasure.'

7

Soon afterwards when Gautier left the soirée with Fiona, he saw
that one of the carriages belonging to the British Embassy was
waiting for them outside. As they drove off, crossing the Seine
and heading for the centre of Paris, he could see Fiona glancing at
him, uneasily it seemed.

'How well do you know Monsieur Wright?' she asked.

'Hardly at all. That was only the second time that we had met.
Why do you ask?'

'He appeared very interested in me. I wonder why.'

'I have no wish to be ungallant and I know nothing about
Monsieur Wright, but my instincts tell me that any interest he
might have in you would be purely political.'

'And is that true of his interest in you as well?'

'Even more so.'

Fiona laughed. 'Then at least we have one thing in common.'

Gautier began to wonder whether he might not have been too
severe in his judgement of Fiona. At any time life must have been
difficult for her: a girl well past her youth, with no suitors and an
eminent father who no doubt treated her with the austere disci-
pline typical of Scottish parents. Then she had suffered the harrowing experience of being exploited and abandoned by a man,

who apparently had not even gone through the motions of seducing her.

Fiona was silent for a time and then she said, 'I learnt today that only a short time ago a very close friend of yours was brutally murdered.'

'Who told you?'

'The Prefect of Police.'

Gautier had not seen her talking to the Prefect at the soirée, but he had no doubt that what she said was true. She went on, 'And if that were not enough, you were then sent off to rescue and bring a silly girl back to Paris. That must have been dreadful for you. I am truly sorry.' She reached out in the darkness and touched his hand.

Looking out of the carriage he saw that they were heading up the Avenue des Champs-Elysées and had passed the turning which would have led them to the British Embassy. 'Are we not going to your embassy?' he asked Fiona.

'No, did I not tell you? While my parents are away the residence is to be completely redecorated. I was offered a room in the apartment of a friend, but I decided to take a room in a hotel. I prefer my privacy.'

Soon afterwards the carriage drew up outside the Hôtel Londonderry. Gautier knew the hotel well and enjoyed excellent relations with the management, so much so that on occasions he had been allowed to spend the night there with one of his mistresses and had not even been sent a bill. He wondered now whether Fiona's choice of the Londonderry had been merely a coincidence.

When he had helped her out of the carriage and they were in the foyer of the hotel she said to him, 'Will you come up to my suite? I can offer you a cognac there.'

Gautier knew now that her choice of hotel had not been a coincidence, but was part of a carefully-laid plan. With that realization came other thoughts. One was a question. Should he object to being the target of her plan? Another was a memory of the brief moment of temptation he had felt when she had lain naked beside him in the cabin on their journey back to France. Then he had been conscious of an obligation to her parents for they had sent him to bring her home. Now there was no obligation. They had left her, a grown woman, alone to do as she wished in a city that was notorious for offering opportunities for sexual adventures. Lastly there was the thought of Ingrid. For how long was he to be conscious of memories of her? To be troubled by feelings of guilt every time he made love to another woman would be ridiculous. He decided he would go up to Fiona's suite and see what happened.

The suite the hotel had given her was on the first floor and Gautier tried to imagine what Fiona might be thinking as they climbed the stairs together. As they reached her suite the door opened and a chambermaid, a small hunched woman, came out. She smiled at them and told Fiona that she had been turning down the sheets in the bedroom. Fiona ignored the woman and did not even return her greeting. In the drawing room a decanter of cognac and two glasses stood on a table and he watched Fiona as she filled one of the glasses.

'Are you not joining me in a cognac?' he asked her.

'No. I think I have may have drunk too much champagne already this evening. I would not like anything to diminish the pleasure I am going to enjoy tonight,' she said, smiling as she handed him the glass.

She took off the wrap she was wearing and crossed the room to drop it over a chair. In Scotland all her movements had seemed awkward and hesitant, but that evening she was self-assured. Gautier wondered whether that was because she was on her own, free of her parents, the 'jailers'. As she came towards him he was aware of her body. When she reached him she took the glass of cognac out of his hands and set it down on the table near them.

'Before you drink that,' she said, 'you will have to answer one question.'

'What question?'

She moved to face him, standing very close and smiling into his eyes. 'Why did you refuse to make love to me on the boat as we crossed the channel?'

'I had a number of reasons, Fiona.'

'It was not because you do not find me attractive, was it?'

'Of course not!'

She took his hands and lifted them to her breasts. Then as he did not take his hands away, she put one hand behind his neck, pulled his face down to hers and kissed him. The kiss was hardly expert, but it was full of passion. Gautier was surprised at the change in her, but could see no reason to resist. Still kissing him, she dropped her hands and with one quick movement slipped the dress she was wearing off her shoulders. She pushed it down over her hips and it fell to the floor, and suddenly she was standing naked in front of him. He realized then that this had been rehearsed, but he did not mind. To be seduced deliberately and with foresight was in a way flattering.

By any standards she could not be described as beautiful, but he could see that the appeal of her body more than compensated for any shortcomings in her facial features. As he gently stroked her breasts, he allowed his other hand to slip down over her waist. He knew then that with her long, slender legs, flat belly and eager hips, making love to her would be an exciting experience; a slow exchange of stimulating caresses leading to the ultimate in satisfaction. He felt himself almost regretting the opportunity he had brushed aside once before.

'Shall we go into the other room?' he asked her, nodding in the direction of the door which he knew led into the bedroom.

'Not yet, chéri. Give me a few more minutes. I want you to be really excited, your lust to be insatiable!'

'Lust' was an odd word to use, Gautier thought, but he supposed it was the fault of her inexperience. Now she began to use her hands, and he felt them slide down over his stomach, stroking his thighs and then reaching into his groin, fumbling for buttons. Gautier felt his control slipping.

'For God's sake, Fiona,' he said hoarsely. 'If we are going to make love let's go to bed!'

She released him and stood back, a mocking smile on her face. 'Not tonight, Jean-Paul.'

'Why not?'

'I have an assignation with another lover who will be here very soon.'

'Another lover? Who?'

'Come now! Surely you did not imagine that you would be the only one who wanted me?'

She turned away, picked up her dress and began putting it on. 'Will you go now, please?' she said and added spitefully, 'and now you know how it feels to be rejected!'

Gautier knew there was nothing he could say. Fiona had one last shot. She said calmly, 'Would you mind leaving by the back stairs? I would hate it if you were to bump into my lover as he arrived.'

Next morning as he was walking from Sûreté headquarters round to the Préfecture de Police, Gautier shook his head and smiled. Had he simply been naïve in allowing Fiona to make a fool of him? He remembered her bitterness when he had refused to make love with her on the steamer returning to France. How could he have supposed that she would so quickly have forgotten that rejection? Few women would. Perhaps his ready acceptance of her sexual advances had been just vanity. It had all happened so quickly, been managed so efficiently. Perhaps he had always seemed to find sexual conquests easy. If that was the case he had been taught a lesson. He remembered her mocking dismissal of him, smiled and shook his head again.

When he reached the Prefect's office he was not surprised to be kept waiting. The Prefect was a busy man and he had recently announced that he was carrying out a major review of all the many regulations and restrictions which affected the daily lives of Parisians. That morning he was in conference, discussing the changes he was proposing to make with senior civil servants in government departments.

When the conference was over and he was admitted to his office, the Prefect said to him, 'Thank you for coming, Gautier.' He pointed to a chair and Gautier knew then that there was something serious to be discussed. 'Tell me, how well do you know the Englishman Wright.'

'Scarcely at all, Monsieur. I have only met him twice: once when he came to my office and once at last night's soirée.'

'Why did he come to your office?'

'It is hard to say. I suspect it was only a fishing trip, to find out how much the police knew about the death of a journalist named Andrassy.'

'Andrassy? He was murdered in Vienna, was he not?'

'Apparently, but he was a regular visitor to Paris.'

The Prefect made no comment and Gautier wondered how much he knew about Andrassy and his relationship with Ingrid. He had often been surprised by what the man knew about a whole range of matters which were not directly the concern of his administration.

'I have a suggestion, Gautier. I think you should make enquiries into the activities of Monsieur Wright; not officially of course.'

'For what should I be looking, Monsieur?'

'Nothing specific. Let me put it this way. Wright has been behaving in a puzzling manner. As you know his function in Paris should merely be to sell the armaments and related products of his company. We would expect him to be making contacts with those people who are in a position to influence decisions to purchase those products: government ministers, their advisers in the civil service, chiefs of staff, generals.'

'I agree.'

'From what I hear, since coming to Paris a few months ago he has spent little time developing such contacts. Almost the only person in government circles with whom he is often seen is Charles Rodier, an official from the École des Beaux Arts who can have little influence on the nation's procurement policies. Apart from that I am told he has been seen more than once with Comte Eugène d'Artagnan.'

The Comte d'Artagnan was a well-known figure in Paris who had created for himself a niche which few would envy. His poems were published in avant-garde reviews and he also wrote scurrilous articles for *La Libre Parole* and other anti-semitic papers. He claimed to be a direct descendant of d'Artagnan, not of the fictitious musketeer but of the old French family, on whom Dumas had based the character in his novel. In spite of this boast he had given little evidence of courage, having fought only one duel and found reasons for refusing several more challenges. His affectation of an effeminate style of dress and his high-pitched voice had led many people to believe he was homosexual.

'That poseur!' Gautier said scornfully.

'Poseur he may be, but we should not underestimate his capacity for mischief. Not long ago we suspected him of playing a leading part in a conspiracy which was aimed at bringing down the government. We could not find any evidence to incriminate him, but he is on my list of dangerous men.'

'What would Wright gain by associating with him?'

'I do not have an answer to that question, which is why I am asking you to make enquiries about what he may be doing. Be discreet though, and it would be better if you did not mention this to your colleagues in the Sûreté.'

Gautier knew that when he said 'colleagues' the Prefect did not mean his fellow officers, but the Director General. Like many people he did not trust Courtrand, who was clearly less concerned with running an efficient police service than with enjoying the perquisites of his office. On more than one occasion he had been known to reveal information which was better kept confidential, only in order to secure himself an invitation to the dining table of a celebrated host.

The Prefect continued talking about Edgar Wright for a little longer, without giving any more information about him or the reasons for his suspicions of the man. Gautier was inclined to believe that he did not have any. He was known to be a man who often acted on flashes of inspiration, or hunches as the Americans now called them, and on the whole they did not fail him. Not only had he remained in office, but he was popular and respected.

As Gautier was leaving he said to him, 'Keep me informed, Gautier, of anything you learn about the Englishman, as a matter of urgency. Feel free to come and see me at any time.'

Gautier had not welcomed the assignment that the Prefect had given him for two reasons. One was because he felt he should be concentrating on solving the problem of Ingrid's murder. Time was slipping away and so far they did not even have a genuine suspect. He knew what had to be done. More men would have to be assigned to the case, routine enquiries begun on a massive scale. They needed to know where Ingrid had spent the evening prior to her death. She would have dined somewhere, either on her own or more probably with someone who might give her a lead on a story which she planned to write. Gautier knew her favourite restaurants, some of which they had visited together. He would make a list of them and that afternoon a policeman would call on every one, trying to establish whether she had dined there that evening and with whom. The drivers of fiacres operating in and around Place des Vosges had already been questioned and now more of them covering a wider area would need to be interviewed. As a last resort pairs of policemen would go knocking on doors, trying to find someone who might have seen or heard a man behaving suspiciously early that morning. It had all been done once, much of it starting when he was in Scotland, but now everything would have to be intensified and it was Gautier who would have to organize the operation.

The second reason why he did not look forward to making enquiries about Edgar Wright was that he did not know where and how to begin. He thought about the matter on his way back to Sûreté headquarters. What the Prefect wanted would mean an investigation into Wright's background as well as a knowledge of his current activities. One would need to know the reason for his appointment to his present post, his previous business career, what resources he had at his disposal, the names of his contacts – business as well as social. All this would have to be established in conditions of secrecy, without him or his friends and colleagues being aware of what was happening. It was not simply a matter of putting the man under surveillance and if it came to that, who could one appoint to watch him?

So he put the problem of Edgar Wright out of his mind and

concentrated on intensifying the investigations into Ingrid's murder. Extra men were taken off other duties, put on the case and briefed. Gautier made a list of the restaurants where he felt Ingrid may have dined, instructions were sent out to the police in other arrondissements which might conceivably become involved. All that took time and when he was satisfied, Gautier knew it was too late to join his friends at the Café Corneille and that he would need to go and have lunch.

On his way out of the building he saw Surat and on an impulse invited him to lunch as well. He liked to take Surat to lunch from time to time for he knew that because of his family commitments, the man could not afford to eat during the day. So giving him a proper lunch was a modest reward for his loyalty and dedication. He also enjoyed his company.

They lunched at a café in Place Dauphine which was only a short walk from the Sûreté headquarters, and where Gautier frequently ate in the evenings as well as at midday. At one time the café had been owned by a widow from Normandy and her daughter Janine. Janine had been Gautier's mistress and he remembered with affection the solace she had brought him. Then she and her mother had gone back to Normandy. A creature of habit, he had continued using the café, even though the cuisine had changed and in his opinion not for the better.

After they had spent several serious minutes discussing what they were going to eat and had placed their orders, Gautier told Surat of the problem he faced in having enquiries made about Edgar Wright. He did not mention that he had been asked to make the enquiries by the Prefect of Police, not because he had been instructed not to inform anyone about the request, but because Surat worked best on direct instructions and his judgement might be clouded if he knew about the top level machinations of the security services.

'Do we know why this Monsieur Wright came to live in Paris?' Surat asked.

'I suppose because he was posted here by his company. As you know his predecessor left under something of a cloud.'

'And where was he working before?'

'In Germany I understand.'

'The police in that country may know something about him.'

Gautier did not point out that a man in Wright's position was unlikely to have a police record.

'Do we know whereabouts in Paris he lives?' Surat asked.

'No, but I could easily find out.'

'Let me know and I will make one of my unofficial visits to the district.'

Surat was talking of the way of collecting information which he sometimes used. In the evenings he would go to the street where the person under surveillance lived and spend an hour or two in the bistros or cafés which his servants were likely to frequent. He would listen to their conversations and after a time they would even let him take part in them, for he appeared to be a pleasant, unassuming fellow whom no one could possibly imagine to be a policeman. Gossiping about their employers was a favourite occupation among servants when they were off duty and they were not averse to sharing their gossip. Using this technique Surat had often been able to pick up useful scraps of information, which he would seldom have gathered by direct questioning.

'If you let me know where Monsieur Wright lives, I could go round there this evening,' Surat suggested.

Gautier's first impulse was to tell Surat not to go, for the man worked longer hours than he was obliged to and should spend more time with his family. Then he reminded himself that only a few minutes earlier he had been reproaching himself for the delays in the investigation of Ingrid's murder, and he was not ready to rule out the possibility that Edgar Wright might in some way be involved.

'I accept your offer,' he told Surat. 'When we return to the Sûreté we will find out exactly where Wright is living.'

Later that afternoon the reports began to come in from the officers who had been checking on the restaurants and cafés where Ingrid might have dined on the evening of her death. They had drawn a blank at most of the restaurants, but the proprietor of one believed that a woman of Ingrid's description had been there in the company of a man. Gautier knew the place and had eaten there from time to time, on one occasion with Ingrid. He felt a frisson of excitement as he read the report, for this was the first hint of a clue which might point towards the identity of Ingrid's killer.

He decided that he would visit the restaurant himself as soon as he had finished work. It was a small, chic establishment on the Left Bank and the people who ate there regularly were mostly drawn from the same social group and known to each other. For this reason the atmosphere was always friendly, with the diners calling out to each other across the room and exchanging banter and flippant remarks. Gautier could well understand that the proprietor, a man from Franche Comté named Claude Piquet, might remember a couple dining there who were not part of the regular clientele.

When he reached the restaurant it was still relatively early and the place was half-empty. Piquet himself had not arrived. When a waiter came up to Gautier he decided on an impulse, to ask for a table. He would have to eat somewhere that evening in any case and that way the waiters and the other diners need not know he was from the police. During the course of his meal he could still ask his questions, preferably of Piquet when he arrived.

After he had ordered his meal he found himself thinking of

Ingrid. The thought that she might have invited the man with whom she had dined back to her apartment still lingered in his mind. He was reluctant to believe it, not through jealousy, but because he refused to think that her death might have been the consequence of some casual sexual adventure.

When Piquet arrived and saw Gautier he came up and welcomed him to the restaurant, making it clear that he remembered him from his previous visits. 'So you are on your own tonight, Monsieur?' he said.

'Sadly yes.'

'I remember that when you dined with us on earlier occasions you were accompanied by charming ladies. One was an American, was she not?'

'Yes, and another was Dutch; a journalist friend of mine.'

Piquet paused, wondering perhaps whether it would be tactful to pursue the matter. Then he said, 'The Dutch lady dined with us not long ago.'

'So I believe. Did you by any chance know her companion?'

Piquet shook his head. 'No. He was not a Frenchman, for they were conversing in another language.'

'German perhaps?'

'No. I would known if it was German.'

Gautier realized that he should have known better than to ask his last question. Piquet's wife, he recalled, came from Lorraine whose neighbouring province was Alsace, where the culture and speech were German in origin. Alsace and Lorraine had been ceded by France to Germany as part of the reparations after the defeat in the Franco-Prussian war. The inhabitants of Lorraine and no doubt Piquet's wife had remained fiercely loyal to France and for that reason hated the Alsatians.

'I cannot be sure but I rather suspect,' Piquet said, 'that he may have come from Italy.'

In a melancholy sort of way Gautier rather enjoyed his dinner that evening. As the restaurant filled up, the atmosphere became lively, reminding him in a way of the Café Corneille, although the conversation and the banter were more earthy and salacious than that of his friends at the café. In a gesture of goodwill Piquet, who had probably guessed he was from the Sûreté, insisted on giving him a glass of a fine old cognac and he lingered over it, in no hurry to return to his empty apartment.

As he walked along the Seine on his way home he decided that his evening had not been wasted. At least he could be fairly certain now of how Ingrid had spent much of the day leading up to her death. Even though Andrassy and Ingrid may have been together for at least the early part of the evening, he could be eliminated as a suspect. They were professional colleagues whose friendship was of long standing and he had no possible reason for wanting to kill her. Walther Kossuth had been a reason for bringing them together and it was on him that Gautier should now concentrate his investigations.

When he arrived back at his apartment, he found that the woman who came in every day to clean for him had left a pile of clothes which she had washed and pressed. He began putting the clothes away for she had been told never to put newly-laundered linen away. Only Gautier knew where everything belonged and he knew that this was a characteristic trait of the fastidious bachelor, which he had now become.

Before he had finished his tidying he heard a knock on the door of the apartment. It was a police officer who had come to tell him that a man had been murdered in Montmartre and that a police wagon was waiting outside to take Gautier to the scene of the crime. The officer did not know the name of the victim but the fact that Gautier had been summoned suggested it must be a person of some importance. Murders were commonplace on almost any evening in or around Pigalle, but the Sûreté was not brought in to deal with the aftermath of knife attacks by jealous pimps or by artists in a drunken frenzy.

At that hour of night it did not take the wagon long to reach Montmartre and soon it drew up outside the Moulin de la Galette. The Moulin de la Galette had originally been one of the windmills that were the feature of Montmartre's hills, but was now a dance hall and the only reminder of its past was an outsize model of a windmill erected in the middle of the dance floor.

By the time Gautier arrived the music had been stopped, but many curious dancers had stayed on to watch the police from the local commissariat, who were questioning anyone who might have seen the incident that had led up to the murder. The body of the murdered man had been taken to the manager's office at the back of the hall and, stretched out on the floor, was being examined by a doctor. The cause of death had been a knife thrust to just below the heart, administered swiftly and expertly even in the confusion of the dance floor and drawing little blood. The face was contorted by a grimace of pain, but that did not prevent Gautier from recognizing the body as that of Comte Eugène d'Artagnan.

8

As soon as he arrived in his office the following morning Gautier wrote a brief report on the death of the Comte d'Artagnan and sent it round by messenger to the office of the Prefect of Police. Only the Prefect could decide whether the murder would in any way compromise the investigations into the activities of Edgar Wright which he had ordered. Gautier's report could merely state the bare facts, because they were all he so far knew about the murder.

The enquiries which he had made at the Moulin de la Galette had told him very little. That a person of the *comte*'s standing should have been at the place at all seemed bizarre. He had been known from time to time to escort some of the fashionable cocottes of Paris to balls and other social events, but this was only to places where they might both benefit from the publicity which would result. This hardly applied to the Moulin de la Galette. No one whom Gautier had questioned had been able to say whether the *comte* had been accompanied by a lady, or a young man, or whether he had been dancing at the time he was stabbed. The people of Montmartre had as always been reluctant to talk to the police and those who might have known something had quickly disappeared when the flics had arrived. More questions would have to be asked among the *comte*'s relatives and regular acquaintances, but this would take time.

He decided that until he heard from the Prefect of Police, he would assign one of the other senior inspectors of the Sûreté to take charge of the routine enquiries into d'Artagnan's murder. In the meantime he would concentrate on that of Ingrid. He had the feeling that there was something in the events leading up to her death which he had overlooked and which none of the officers engaged on the case were likely to uncover.

Thinking of Ingrid he remembered how he had allowed Fiona to play at seducing him at the Hôtel Londonderry. At the time he had brushed away any pang of guilt he might have felt by the thought that life must go on. Ingrid herself, with her knowledge of life and her scorn of sentimentality, would not have reproached him for giving way to the temptation of the moment, but even so. . . .

Now he deliberately sidestepped the issue of guilt by telling himself that there were aspects of Fiona's 'elopement' to Scotland which had to be addressed. Ingrid and Andrassy may have planned to meet discuss Walther Kossuth, presumably because Andrassy had learned something newsworthy about the Hungarian. Soon afterwards they had both been murdered and one did not need much imagination to wonder whether they had died because they had unwittingly become involved in some polit-ical intrigue in the Balkans.

Then there was Edgar Wright. Why had Wright shown such an interest in Fiona and in her journey to Scotland? Finally there been the murder of d'Artagnan in a seedy Montmartre dance hall. The Prefect of Police had hinted that d'Artagnan was a dangerous man. All three murders would have to be investigated, but Gautier felt that he was inhibited by the instructions that the Prefect had given him. He still felt a dull anger at the death of Ingrid, and while he knew that he must not let that anger give way to a desire for revenge, he felt frustrated by the inaction which had been

110

imposed on him. All he could do was to sit in his office and wait for the Prefect's response to the report he had sent him.

He did not wait. When the middle of the day approached he left his office, crossed to the Left Bank and began heading for the Café Corneille. As he walked along Boulevard Saint Germain his mood changed, the slight feeling of depression which usually accompanied inactivity lifting to be replaced by anticipation. The conversation of his friends at the café, even on the trivial issues of the day, was always stimulating.

That day he must have been earlier than usual in arriving, for he found only two of the regulars at the café: the elderly judge and Froissart the bookseller. Froissart was telling the judge of a manuscript he had been sent by a young author who was hoping to have it published. Although the proposed book was intended to be a review of current trends in painting, much of it was based on the life of Misia Edwards. Misia was the wife of Alfred Edwards, one of the wealthiest men in France and for that reason one of the most powerful. Although she was already married, Edwards had persuaded her first to become his mistress, and after they had both divorced, to marry him. Now although they had been married for little more than two years, rumour had it that he was pursuing a well-known actress and that another divorce was not far off.

Froissart explained that the book would not be a story of Misia's unconventional domestic life, but on her role as a patron of the arts. She had been painted by several of the leading artists of the day, including Vuillard, Bonnard, Toulouse-Lautrec and Renoir. He was worried nevertheless that the book might contain passages that could be interpreted as defamatory and he was asking the judge for advice on this issue.

'I am hardly in a position to cross swords with Alfred Edwards,' he said.

'I would not worry too much on that account,' the judge told him. 'There can be few laws in France or indeed anywhere, which are treated with such contempt as that of libel. Every newspaper feels free to publish the most scurrilous accusations on eminent people. Scarcely a day passes without our leading actors and actresses being grossly maligned, not to mention the President of the Republic. Would you not agree, Gautier?'

'Fortunately we police officers are not paid to interpret the law, but to enforce it,' Gautier replied, 'but do not all good Americans believe that one should publish and be damned?'

The conversation continued in the same light-hearted vein. Presently the young lawyer arrived, but he refused to be drawn into the discussion. His opinion, he said, would be too expensive. When they saw Duthrey come into the café, the others realized that he too, as a firm believer in the sanctity of marriage and family life, was unlikely to take part in the flippant debate. They were right but for a different reason.

Almost as soon as he joined them at their table he told the others excitedly, 'The Comte d'Artagnan is dead.'

'Dead!'

'Yes. He was killed in a brawl at a dance hall.'

As he was speaking Duthrey looked uneasy. By tacit agreement the friends at the Café Corneille never discussed any criminal or other police matters in case they might put Gautier in a difficult position. What he had now said was hardly a major gaffe, but Gautier decided to spare him any embarrassment.

'What Duthrey says is true,' he said, 'or so I understand. I am not involved in the affair myself.'

The half-truth achieved what he had hoped it would and the members of their group began talking about the murder of d'Artagnan. Most of what they said was no more than speculation, since the murder had happened too late to be covered in the day's newspapers. Duthrey himself had only heard of it as reports from Montmartre began coming into his office. The affair was never going to be a sensation and the interest it aroused in the café that day was only because of d'Artagnan's notoriety. People began recalling other occasions when the man had shocked society: one was when he had announced that he intended to marry the Valtesse de la Bigne, an elderly cocotte who had been the mistress of Napoleon III; another was when he had somehow managed to find his way on to the stage of *l'Opera* during a performance of *Tristan et Isolde*, from where he had begun a rousing speech in favour of homosexuality.

The stir caused by the news of d'Artagnan's murder did not last for long that day, because those who met at the Café Corneille were men of wider interests.

Presently discussion moved on to politics and was polarized into debate by the arrival of the deputy for Seine-et-Marne who, as usual, threw out little scraps of information on controversial issues.

Gautier was enjoying the good-tempered debate and had put all the three murders out of his mind, when he noticed three new arrivals coming into the café. As they walked past the table at which his group were sitting one of the men nodded to him, and he realized then that it was the representative of the English armaments company, Edgar Wright. He could not recall ever having seen either of Wright's companions before.

The deputy for Seine-et-Marne, who had noticed Wright's nod, remarked to Gautier, 'I see that you know the Englishman who has ambitions to rearm our country.'

'I have met him, yes.'

'I wonder what business he could possibly have with our École des Beaux Arts.'

'Monsieur?'

'One of the men with him is Charles Rodier.'

'The civil servant?' Froissart asked.

'I suppose you could call him a civil servant, though he would not take that as a compliment. He is an accountant whom the Government appointed to keep an eye on the finances of the École.'

'And the other man?'

'I believe his name is Dorval and he comes of a good family. I gather he has just returned to France from the colonies.'

On his way back to Sûreté headquarters Gautier wondered why Edgar Wright had gone to the Café Corneille that morning. He could not believe it had been just by coincidence that Wright and Rodier had appeared at the café together. Wright could easily have found out that Gautier frequently visited the café to meet his friends before lunch, but what motive could he have had for taking Rodier there with him?

When he reached Sûreté headquarters he found a note from the Prefect of Police waiting for him. It was headed PRIVATE AND CONFIDENTIAL and it read:

Gautier. The murder of d'Artagnan changes the situation and you must obviously investigate it in the usual way. However, please follow my instructions with regard to EW as far as you are able. I find it hard to believe he could be involved in the murder. Keep me informed.

Back at Sûreté headquarters Gautier found Surat waiting for him, but there was nothing in his manner to suggest that he had any news of importance. He told Gautier that in a back number of *Le Matin* he had found an account of a ball given by the Duchesse de Trèves, the timing of which made it possible that this was the ball at which Fiona may have met Walther Kossuth. The British

Ambassador, together with his wife and daughter, was listed among the guests at the ball, but there was no mention of anyone named Kossuth.

'This fellow Kossuth is proving very elusive,' Gautier complained. 'What I would like to know is why he was so keen to leave France. What had he done? And why did he want to go to Ireland?'

Surat had no answers to those questions, but he had one other piece of news for Gautier. 'Did you know, *patron*, that you are being watched?'

'Watched?'

'Followed might be a better word. There was a man waiting opposite the Sûreté building this morning and when you left he followed you.'

'Have you any idea who he might be?'

'None. I have seen him before, loitering by the stalls of the *bouquinistes* along the river, but I did not realize until today that he was there to spy on you.'

Gautier remembered then having on occasions felt that he was being followed, but he had laughed at the idea. Who would be so stupid as to follow a policeman? 'If you are sure of this,' he told Surat, 'and if you see him there again bring him in for questioning. If you must, arrest him.'

After Surat had left he found himself thinking that although several days had elapsed since Ingrid had been found dead, virtually no progress had been made in solving her murder. Could that be, he wondered, because he was too close to it, too personally involved? He dismissed the thought. Only that morning when he awoke he had reproached himself with a pang of guilt for allowing Ingrid to drift out of his consciousness. The pain he had known when he knew she was dead had slowly been diluted and other feelings had begun to take its place.

He was still brooding over this when Inspector Fénelon came into the room. Fénelon was the man he had assigned to handle the murder of the Comte d'Artagnan. He had the air of a man bringing good news.

'I thought you would wish to know, Chief Inspector, that the scoundrel who stabbed the *comte* has been arrested.'

'Who was it?'

'A local man named Magnol who has been in trouble more than once before.'

'And his motive?'

'Money. We found the money he had been paid to kill the *comte* in his home.'

'That was careless of him. How did you find out he was the murderer?'

'An informer told us; one of his friends strangely enough.'

Gautier was surprised. For many years Montmartre had been the home of villains and petty crooks. That dated back to the time when the *butte* lay outside the old city walls and those who lived there felt themselves safe from surveillance by the police. Only in recent times had struggling artists, their models and their mistresses gone to live and work there. They had given the district a veneer of respectability, but the old traditions of a criminal society lingered. No one would even go to help an injured policeman lying in the street and anyone acting as an informer to the flics would not have long to live.

'I would be interested to know who paid the informer,' Gautier said. 'You think he was bought?'

'Almost certainly. First one pays a scoundrel to stab the comte d'Artagnan and then to tidy matters up, one pays another to give us his name and send him to the guillotine. An expensive operation no doubt, but neat in a way: two two dead men for the price of one.'

On the following Monday Gautier went into his office even earlier than usual. His Sunday had not been one to enjoy, a day during most of which boredom had wrestled with dissatisfaction and not successfully. There had been none of the small pleasures which for much of his life he had associated with Sundays: no leisurely meals in relaxing company, no escape from Paris to eat and take a glass of wine in a country *guinguette* on the banks of the Seine, not even the company of an attractive woman. Was life passing him by, he had asked himself, or was he just growing old, taking the first steps on a journey from which there was no return?

Back in his office even the routine work which waited for him seemed duller than usual. There were the reports of petty crimes, the complaints of English and American visitors who had strayed from the comparative safety of the great boulevards into dubious red light areas, where they had allowed themselves to be tricked – swindled would be too strong a word – out of a few pounds or dollars. He dealt with the reports as swiftly as they deserved, writing laconic words of instruction on each.

He had almost finished working through all the reports when a message arrived for him from Dublin. Soon after returning from Scotland he had been in touch with the Irish Constabulary, asking them whether they had any information on Kossuth and this was their answer. Kossuth was in Ireland, travelling with a passport that seemed to be in order. He appeared to have contacts among a group of dissident Irishmen whose professed objective was to free their country from British rule, but had done nothing for which he might be detained and questioned.

The constabulary would keep a check on his movements and inform the Sûreté of any developments.

Nothing he had learned so far about Kossuth indicated that he could have been involved in Ingrid's murder, so clutching at straws, he decided that he should question the man who had been arrested for killing d'Artagnan and who was being held in the police commissariat of the 18th arrondissement, until he could be charged by a magistrate and lodged in a more secure prison. Before leaving the Sûreté he left a message for Inspector Fénelon who was now working on another investigation, telling him what he planned to do.

Jules Magnol appeared to be typical of the louts to be found in and around Montmartre, as well as in any other districts where men, without scruples and more importantly without any talents, scratched a living out of petty crime or pimping or both. He was also a man of little spirit who now, having in effect confessed to killing the Comte d'Artagnan, had resigned himself to what he knew would await him: the guillotine.

Gautier spoke to him, asking him questions about himself which he answered readily enough, as though conversation provided a welcome distraction. One question Gautier did not ask him was who had paid him to stab d'Artagnan. There might be other ways of arriving at that particular truth. So they talked about Magnol's wife, her parents who had never thought him good enough for her and who would take her back when he was gone.

Slowly and at first reluctantly, Magnol began to answer his questions. His wife, he admitted, was a good woman and deserved more than he had ever given her. She would be all right, for her parents were a solid bourgeois couple who would look after her and their one son. He himself had not given them much, but what could a man do? Since he had never been taught a trade, he had always had to rely on casual work. What little money he had been able to earn had never done more than pay the bare expenses of living. Gautier listened with some sympathy, for he understood the predicament in which many men living in that part of Paris found themselves.

As he talked about money, Magnol's attitude changed. One sensed that he was thinking of the money he had been paid to murder d'Artagnan, which may well have been a larger sum than had ever passed through his hands before and he could not resist boasting about it. That money could have brought his family greater security than they had ever known. He needed only a little prompting to complain about how it had been found by the police and taken away from him. The man who had betrayed him, the informer, had been a friend. Brisset and he had shared many adventures, been drunk together. How could he have sold him to the authorities?

'Who provided the money?' Gautier asked him. 'You may as well tell me now.'

Magnol's first impulse was obviously to refuse. He had been brought up among people who hated and distrusted the flics, but perhaps because he knew he had been betrayed by one of them and a friend of his at that, his loyalty had been weakened.

He shrugged. 'I do not know the name of the man. He was not from the Butte, but still a Frenchman and well spoken.'

'Would you recognize him if you saw him again?'

'Probably, although he approached me at night, outside a café.'

After Magnol had been taken back to his cell, Gautier spoke to the officer at the 18th arrondissement who was in charge of the murder enquiry. He admitted that Brisset was known to the police. Now they would have to find out who had paid him to inform on Magnol. Little by little, with patient and, if needed, aggressive questioning, the truth would be established even though it would come too late to save Magnol. Whether the trail would ever lead to the man or men who had been responsible for having d'Artagnan murdered remained to be seen.

When he returned to the Sûreté, he found Surat waiting for him and he could tell from his manner that he had news. 'Do you remember, *patron*, what I told you about a man whom I thought was spying on you last week? Well, he was waiting outside again this morning, ready to follow you. I had him picked up and brought in for questioning.'

'What did he have to say for himself?'

'After a little forceful persuasion he admitted that he had been paid to watch you and report back on your movements.'

'Did he say by whom?'

Surat smiled. 'Finally, yes, after he had been frightened into an admission. Apparently he is on the payroll of a civil servant, Charles Rodier. Would you believe it, a civil servant? What is the world coming to when civil servants spy on us?'

'Rodier is not exactly a civil servant. He is an accountant.'

'One should not be surprised. Only an accountant would employ such a useless creature.'

9

As he was in the employ of the Government, learning the basic facts about Charles Rodier was not difficult. Originally from Lille, his date of birth, place of education, marital status and salary could all be established from public records. Wishing to know more about a man who might be involved in a criminal conspiracy, Gautier decided to tap another source of information. Daniel Nogaret was an official in the Ministry of Finance whom he had known for many years. At one time they had been close friends for Gautier's wife Suzanne had been to the same school as Nogaret's wife. After both their wives had died, the two men had kept in touch, but only spasmodically, for both had other interests and Nogaret had remarried. When Gautier telephoned him that morning, he readily agreed that they should lunch together.

They met in a café just off Boulevard de la Madeleine, which one could tell immediately was frequented mainly by civil servants, for the whole place had an authoritative air. It was not that the officials in the café did not gossip as Gautier's friends in the Café Corneille did, but they did so with restraint, hinting that they had state secrets which could not be revealed. As Gautier and Nogaret shared a demi-carafe of wine, they talked of the past, but without nostalgia. Nogaret did not seem surprised that Gautier

had not married for a second time. As he put it, the life of a policeman with its irregular hours and brushes with violence, was not one which many women would wish to share. His own second marriage had worked out well, bringing him a battalion of new relations whose company and affection, rather to his surprise, he enjoyed.

They lunched in a small café not far away, where there were no civil servants and where they could talk freely. When Gautier began asking questions about Rodier, Nogaret did not seem surprised, which made Gautier wonder whether others beside himself were showing an interest in the accountant.

'Like many senior men in government service,' Nogaret said, 'Rodier has a private income.'

'A substantial income?'

'Large enough to have allowed him for several years to indulge his lifestyle.'

'And that is?'

'He is a poseur. All his life he has tried to think of himself as a man about town; acting the part of a wealthy clubman, going to the races, playing the tables, fighting duels supposedly in defence of some woman's honour, being seen in the same exclusive brothels as the Prince of Wales was supposed to patronize.'

'And did he ever marry?'

'Never. He still keeps a *garçonniere*, but merely as a front, because I know of no woman who has ever been entertained there. Except one, that is.'

'And who was she?'

'He was rash enough to start a liaison with a young girl; one of the students at the École des Beaux Arts. Her parents got to know of it and complained. The scandal nearly cost Rodier his position, but he had powerful friends in the government who saved him.'

'What do you know about her?' Gautier asked.

'Very little. They say she wanted more than Rodier was able to give her, and I am not talking of money. All this happened years ago; fifteen years or even more. As soon as the scandal broke her parents took her home from Paris. Her name was Lottie, which is a German name they tell me.'

'You say Rodier has powerful friends. Does he have any political influence?'

'He had at one time if only for his wealth and contacts. I have no wish to seem cynical, but politicians can be bought the same as anyone else.'

'You are talking of the past. Are you saying that his political influence has declined?'

'I believe it has,' Nogaret said, 'as has his wealth. I am not saying he is in financial straits, but he is in less evidence at those occasions when the rich flaunt their money. As we say in France he is no longer a man of the highest standing.'

There was nothing more Nogaret could tell him about Rodier's private life and they began talking about other matters. As so often happened they turned to the subject of war, the war with Germany which many Frenchmen believed was inevitable, for the humiliations of the last war could never be forgotten or forgiven. Gautier had noticed that it was mostly men with a contented domestic life who were pessimistic about France's political future. He steered the conversation back to a personal level and for the rest of the lunch he listened to stories of the happiness which Nogaret's new family had brought him.

He walked all the way back to Sûreté headquarters, heading first for Place de la Concorde and then cutting across the Jardin des Tuileries. Walking, he always found, stimulated his analytical faculties, giving him the time and mental space he needed to place one thought upon another carefully and precisely and so construct a viable idea. On that day his thinking was not productive.

On the surface it appeared that Rodier no longer carried enough influence with the French Government to influence its decisions on the purchase of arms. If he were playing any part in the negotiations, Gautier felt it must be a minor one. Even so there were still disquieting aspects of the strategy Edgar Wright was using in the whole affair. After reflection Gautier decided it would be best to forget about Rodier, at least for the time being, and to concentrate on Wright himself.

When he reached his office, he sent for Surat and told him what little he knew about Edgar Wright and where he lived. Because he sensed that Gautier wanted enquiries conducted with some urgency, Surat volunteered to make his first expedition to the district that evening. Knowing what demands evening work must make on the man's family life, Gautier knew he should have told him to wait until the following day or even until later in the week, but he did not.

Soon after Surat had left his office, a messenger came up from the ground floor bringing a *petit bleu*, or message sent over Paris's pneumatic telegraph system, which had arrived for Gautier. It read: 'Inspector Gautier. My duties have brought me to Paris for a time. Is there any chance that we might meet? Sylvie Lambert.'

The following evening Gautier dined with Sylvie Lambert at Piquet's restaurant. He had replied to her *petit bleu* with one of his own, sent to the address she had given at the Ministry for Foreign Affairs and inviting her to dine with him. One reason for his invitation was that he wished to repay her for all the help she had given him in London. Another reason was a feeling that she might know something about Edgar Wright which he had been unable to learn in Paris. In London she had told him that the French Embassy worked closely with the British authorities on questions of immigration. He supposed it was possible that they had been consulted by the French authorities when Wright had been sent by his company to live in Paris. A third reason was that he enjoyed her company. He had chosen Piquet's restaurant because he thought Sylvie would appreciate its ambience of elegant informality, and he was waiting at the table they had been given when she arrived.

As he kissed her hand, she said, smiling, 'I am not sure that I should have accepted your invitation.'

'Why not?'

'Before you left London for Scotland you promised that on you way back you would take me out to dinner.'

'Circumstances prevented me from stopping in London on my way back to France.'

'Circumstances? Or was it the charms of the diplomat's daughter?' she asked, teasing him.

Gautier remembered his promise and her comment when he had made it. 'And am I forgiven now that you are dining with me?'

'Possibly, but I shall expect all your usual gallantry and attention.'

'You shall have it, I promise.'

'More promises?'

They both laughed. At the table, while they were taking an aperitif, Sylvie explained why she was in Paris. It was customary for French diplomats to spend only a limited time in any country to which they had been posted. When they had completed a tour they were not posted immediately to another country, but spent a time in France, which was in effect a period of retraining, giving them an opportunity to acquaint themselves with developments in government policy and in the thinking of the Ministry for Foreign Affairs. Now, Sylvie told Gautier, the same arrangement was being used for senior members of staff in foreign missions.

125

'Does this mean that you will be spending some months in France?' Gautier asked her.

'Probably two years at the very least. It will give me a chance to see my family in the Dordogne.'

'But you will be working in Paris?'

Sylvie nodded.

'So that means we can spend more time together?'

'I hope so.'

There was nothing flirtatious in the remark. Gautier saw Sylvie smile as she glanced at him and he seemed to see humour in her smile. He realized that Sylvie was an example of a new generation of modern young women who, while they might not see themselves as the equal of men, were at least ready to dispense with the old rigid conventions of social behaviour and would expect men to do the same. So he did not attempt to advise her on her choice of dishes from the menu that evening and together they selected the wine they would drink.

After they had ordered, she looked round the restaurant. 'Do you eat here regularly?' she asked him.

'Not often. To enjoy Piquet's one should be with friends. Here a solitary diner feels, I don't know how to put it, exposed.'

'The place is so very Parisian; the real Paris, not a place for rich English and American visitors. This is the Paris I have missed so much in England. Of course I read all the Paris newspapers, but that is not the same. For one thing I am always two or even three days behind.'

'Then while you are here, we will have to make sure that you hear all the gossip and all the scandals,' Gautier said smiling.

'Only the other day I enjoyed reading in the papers of a typical occasion of Paris society: a soirée in the home of the Duchesse de Nièvre.'

'As it happens I was there.'

'So? You are invited to these grand affairs?'

'You need not sound so surprised! As an unattached man I was simply invited to make up the numbers.'

'I cannot believe that.'

'It is true.'

Gautier told Sylvie of the *duchesse*'s invitation to Verlaine. She laughed and told him a story of her own, which was one about the Prince de Saint-Auban, long acknowledged to be the leader of *Tout Paris*, the highest echelon of Paris society. When he awoke each morning the Prince, so it was rumoured, was brought a cup of chocolate laced with cognac and the day's newspapers. He would then read the obituaries and if his name were not among them, would return to bed, sleep for another hour, rise and eat a champagne breakfast before going riding in the Bois.

'Like the Prince,' Sylvie commented, 'I am sure you have many fruitful years left.'

'Perhaps,' Gautier replied, 'and if so I hope you will allow me to spend at least a part of them in your company.'

'Only if you do not tease me with empty promises.'

Gautier decided that the way in which their conversation was developing had opened the way for him to raise a question he wished to ask her. 'One of the guests at that soirée,' he told her, 'was an Englishman, Edgar Wright.'

'The representative of the armament company Lydon-Walters?'

'Yes. What do you know about Wright?'

'A little. Before being posted to France he was the company's top man in Germany. I am told he was brilliantly successful there. I also met him once at a reception which his company gave for French officials living in London. I imagine that was his way of introducing himself to the French before he came here.'

'So he sold the Prussians all the rifles and artillery they could use and now he has come to put France on a war footing; playing one side against the other.'

'That is his *métier*.'

Gautier realized that Sylvie would have a diplomat's impartiality and would see nothing wrong in Edgar Wright selling arms to both sides in what might well be a prelude to war. By the same token she would probably not mind if she were asked a direct question about Wright's connections.

'Do you know if Wright has ever had any dealings with Austria or the Balkans?'

'I have no idea, but I can try to find out.'

'I would not wish to put you to any trouble.'

'In diplomacy we thrive on trouble.' Sylvie smiled. 'And when I have the answer to your question it will give me an excuse to see you again.'

'Mademoiselle, you need never find excuses to do that.'

'For an Englishman, Monsieur Edgar Wright has become accepted in Paris very quickly,' Surat said.

The following morning he had arrived at Gautier's office to report on the evenings he had spent in and around the district where Wright had his apartment.

As always he had found no difficulty in making friends with the ordinary people in the *quartier*. All those who worked for Wright had agreed that he was a good employer, not too demanding, considerate and fair.

'You heard nothing against him?'

'Nothing of any substance. One of his servants has a cousin in Germany and she hinted that he was a *pédé*.'

'A homosexual?'

'That was what she suggested, but it was no more than servants' gossip and not all of his other staff agreed with her.'

128

Although homosexual practices were not proscribed by law, as a nation the French disapproved strongly of pederasty, seeing it as a betrayal of manliness and a draining of virility, and it was regarded with scorn and derision. Many believed that it had contributed to the country's ignominious defeat by the Prussians three decades earlier. At the same time many Frenchmen were convinced that in Germany homosexuality was now widely practised.

Only that year a homosexual scandal had broken involving Kaiser Wilhelm II, when two of his closest friends had been accused by a boatman and a milkman of having homosexual relations with them. The accusations were never proved, but the case had caused such a scandal that the Kaiser had been obliged to end his friendship with them. Before that incident the German arms magnate Krupp was alleged to have committed suicide to avoid being expelled from Capri for corrupting young boys on the island. The French had been delighted and gleeful graffiti celebrating the discomfort of the hated enemy had appeared on the walls of many of the *pissotières* of Paris.

'Did you learn anything about Wright's friends and contacts?' Gautier asked Surat. 'A man in his business must entertain frequently in his home.'

'Oh, he does. His staff say he has guests to dinner almost every evening. That is one grumble they have.'

'Do any of the guests go regularly?'

'The man Rodier does. You know about him of course. Many of the other guests, I was told, are well-known people: deputies, senior civil servants, journalists. Rodier usually goes on his own, but on one occasion he took as his guest a woman with whom he seemed to be on very intimate terms. The staff say she behaved rather badly, drank too much, made a scene.'

'What happened?'

129

'Nothing much. One of the other guests was sorry for her and took her home in a fiacre.'

Gautier told Surat that he had done well in his backstairs enquiries and that another evening spent in the *quartier* might be well worthwhile. He had only one more question to ask him. 'Do you know if the Comte d'Artagnan was ever a guest at Wright's home?'

'I thought that you might ask that. There was bad blood between the two men and it seems that Wright's staff had orders never to admit the *comte*. There was quite a stir when they heard that he had been murdered,' Surat replied. Then he added, 'Wright could not have killed him because he was home on the night of the murder, entertaining guests. I checked.'

Gautier restrained a smile. He admired Surat's thoroughness but found it amusing that he had even thought Wright might have gone up to Montmartre and stabbed the man himself. Before he left Gautier's office Surat remembered one more fact that he had learned from Wright's servants.

'They have one other cause for complaint which I have not mentioned,' he said. 'Apparently Wright has one guest staying at this apartment permanently; a man named François Dorval. They say he has just returned to France from the colonies and has all the worst habits of the colonial settlers. He is arrogant and a bully and treats the servants as though it was his own apartment.'

'Did they know anything about him?'

'Not really. The servants think he must be short of funds. It seems that every time he arrives at the apartment he makes the servants pay for the fiacre.'

Surat left but was away for only a matter of minutes and when he returned he was carrying a sheet of paper which, he explained, carried the names of the journalists who had attended the meeting of the press arranged by the Ministry for Foreign Affairs.

'But that was days, almost weeks ago!' Gautier said.

130

'The list has only just arrived. You know what these *petits fonctionnaires* are like. They thrive on procrastination.'

Gautier looked at the list and saw the names of Ingrid and Neuhoff were on it, but not that of Luca Marinetti. He pointed this out to Surat who said, 'That must be an error, unless of course Marinetti forgot to sign the sheet. These things happen.'

A tiny glimmer of suspicion flickered in Gautier's mind. He had asked for the list only because he had wondered whether Ingrid might have met someone at the press conference and been involved in some incident, which later had led to her murder. Now the fact that Marinetti might have lied when he had claimed to have been at the conference made him curious.

'Maybe,' he said. 'Go round to Rue Réaumur and find out whether he was in fact at the press conference. If he is not at the office, one of the other journalists may be able to confirm what he told me.'

Surat was gone for not much more than an hour. While he was away Gautier was not thinking of Marinetti or the press conference, for there were other matters to occupy his mind. News had come of a major collapse in law and order in Marseille. This had been triggered off initially by a demonstration outside a major bank. Customers of the bank, hearing a rumour that it was on the edge of insolvency and that their funds were to be transferred to Paris, had assembled to demand reassurance. When this was not forthcoming they had broken into the bank's premises, raided the strongroom and begun seizing whatever cash and valuables they could find. The police had intervened and a major riot had developed in the streets, involving thousands of people who had originally been drawn to the scene simply by curiosity. The citizens of Marseille were independent and always truculent, ready to defy authority on any excuse. The Sûreté in Paris was not involved, but had been placed on alert as a precaution.

When Surat returned, he told Gautier that Marinetti was not in the journalists' office at Rue Réaumur. Neuhoff had been there and he had told Surat that the Italian had not attended the press conference of the Ministry for Foreign Affairs. He had been emphatic about this. Only he and Ingrid had been there.

'Then what is this man Marinetti up to?' Gautier asked.

'I do not know, *patron*. They say he has disappeared.'

'Disappeared?'

'He has not been to the offices in Rue Réaumur for some days. Rumour has it that he was last seen boarding a train for Vienna.'

'Vienna? I thought he came from Italy.'

'He claims to be Italian, but who knows?'

10

The investigations into Luca Marinetti which were begun that afternoon brought a number of surprises. His colleagues at Rue Réaumur confessed to knowing little about the man. He had moved into the office only a few weeks previously, having rented from the owners of the building the desk, which had become vacant when another Italian was said to have been recalled by his paper in Milan. The other three journalists evidently had not been as inquisitive as journalists are supposed to be and did not even know where in Paris Marinetti lived, whether he was married or for what other newspapers he may have worked. When questioned they admitted never having seen him typing at his desk nor sending a telegram. A quick study of recent copies of leading Italian papers showed no stories appearing over his name. Gautier had formed the impression that the man was typically Italian: handsome, charming and well-mannered, though not, one would have thought, industrious or totally dedicated to the newspaper business. More information about the man and his background would no doubt be unearthed by Surat and a team of police officers, but that would need time and a good deal of work.

In the meantime Charles Rodier had been placed under surveillance; only the loosest surveillance, for Gautier doubted whether he could be playing a significant part in any conspiracy. One thing which surprised him was that the Prefect of Police was not pressing for action. He appeared, for the time being at least, to have lost interest in Wright. The Prefect, as everyone knew, was a man of many varied interests and perhaps he might now be concentrating on enlivening the life of some lonely widow.

By the end of the afternoon information about Marinetti began to percolate in to the Quai des Orfèvres, so much information indeed that it became clear Marinetti was not bothering to cover his tracks after his disappearance. He was discovered to have been living in an apartment which he had rented by the quarter, and Gautier could not help observing that the apartment was not far from the Marais where Ingrid had been living. When the police called, all the owner would say was that the Italian had left without warning and without saying where he was going. The apartment had not for the time being been relet and Gautier arranged for police officers to be sent round to search it, even though he was not hopeful that they would find anything of any significance.

Before his suspicions about what the Italian might have been doing had taken tangible shape, the telephone in his office rang. The call was from Corbin, the secretary of the Director General, telling him that Courtrand wished to see him as a matter of urgency. Gautier went upstairs, wearily, for whenever Courtrand decided to take a hand in the running of the Sûreté, his interference was almost always ineffective and could be disastrous.

When he went into Courtrand's office, he was shocked by his appearance. The man, who had been away from his office for several days, looked grey and pinched and drained of all vitality. In spite of that, his first words showed that he still had some spirit in him.

'What is this I hear, Gautier,' he said. 'Is it true that you have been pestering the daughter of the British Ambassador?'

'Monsieur?'

'Did you not escort her home after a recent soirée given by the Duchesse de Nièvre?'

'Only because she asked me to. Her mother and father were away in England.'

'And was the Prefect of Police aware of what you were doing? I am told he was also at the soirée.'

Now Gautier saw the purpose of Courtrand's questions. He had learnt that Gautier had been seen speaking to the Prefect at the soirée and knew that from time to time the Prefect approached Gautier without consulting Courtrand, and even going over his head. He was not in a position to object to their relationship but understandably wished to be aware of any initiatives they might be taking.

Gautier decided to give him a slightly dishonest answer. 'The Prefect is concerned about the murder of the Comte d'Artagnan.' Courtrand paused, perhaps restraining the comment which he would have liked to have made. Then he said, 'And you Gautier. I trust that you are not wasting too much time on the death of that shabby little nonentity.' As Gautier made no reply, he continued, 'In my opinion whoever stabbed d'Artagnan was doing society a service. We shall find out who it was eventually. And in the meantime, apart from the ambassador's daughter, what is occupying your time?'

'We are still investigating the murder of Madame Van de Velde. A journalist colleague of hers named Marinetti has disappeared.' Gautier could see no harm in telling Courtrand at least a little of the truth.

'Marinetti?' Courtrand exclaimed. 'Surely you do not suspect him of killing your *petite amie*? One must admit though that the man is exceptionally good-looking.'

Gautier sighed inwardly, but that was all. Courtrand was not known for either tact or subtlety. He went on, 'In the meantime, Gautier, there is another matter I have to raise with you. The commissariat has informed me that you still have not accounted for the expenses you incurred on your little jaunt across the Channel.'

Evidently Courtrand had lost interest in Marinetti and for the next twenty minutes he tried to provoke Gautier into arguing over a number of trivial issues connected with the administration of the Sûreté. As he walked back to his own office, Gautier found himself thinking that the man's powers of concentration had rapidly declined. This was no doubt the result of his recent illness and one had to wonder whether the deterioration would continue and if so how that would affect the well-being of the whole department.

In the normal way Courtrand would probably have retired from his post in four or five years, but one could not rule out the possibility that he might be obliged to leave earlier, in which case a new Director General would have to be found. Courtrand's appointment had been, as happened so often in France, a piece of patronage, a return for favours he had done for leading politicians or top figures in the administration. Who would replace him? Gautier and the other senior officers of the Sûreté had learned to live with Courtrand's vanity, petulance and occasional bungling interference. Any successor might be more difficult to contain: more autocratic, more self-important and, what would be worse, even more interfering.

The frustration of dealing with Courtrand had left Gautier restless. He told himself that he was spending too much time in his office. Efficient police work needed more than giving directions and reading reports. He should be spending more time in those areas of the city where crimes were being committed.

Remembering that earlier in the afternoon he had sent police officers to search the apartment where Marinetti had been living, he
decided that he would go round there himself and see what
progress they were making.

The apartment building was in the 11th arrondissement, not
too far from either the Gare de l'Est or the Gare du Nord, if one
were wishing to leave Paris in a hurry. The door of the building
was opened to him by a woman of barely thirty who would have
been pretty but for her red, tear-filled eyes. Explaining that she
was Madame Julie, the wife of the owner who was out, she told
him that two policemen were still searching Marinetti's apartment.

'Why are they here?' she asked 'What has our tenant done? Is
he not returning here?'

'Where can we talk, Madame?' Gautier replied.

She led him into what must be the living room of her husband
and herself. There he asked her a string of questions. How long
had Marinetti been occupying his apartment? Was he single? Did
she know what he did for a living? From what part of Italy did he
come? Had he always paid for his apartment promptly? Did he
entertain and if so what kind of guests did he invite home with
him? Had she any idea where he might have gone? She appeared
to be answering honestly enough and it was only when he began
questioning her about any guests whom Marinetti might have
entertained in his apartment that she could no longer restrain her
tears.

'He is a good man,' she said, sobbing, 'not a womanizer like
many of our tenants. He spends many of his evenings alone.
Sometimes when my husband was out, I took pity on him and
would carry him up some food. He always offered me a glass of
wine and we would have long chats. Now I suppose I will never
see him again.'

'What makes you think that?' Gautier asked.

'He left two days ago without telling me where he was going. That was not like him.'

'Has he paid his rent?'

'Of course. As always for three months ahead.'

'And you have no idea where he may have gone?'

'None. He must have left in a hurry,' Madame Julie said tearfully, 'for he has left many of his clothes and other possessions behind.'

Leaving her Gautier went up to the apartment which Marinetti had occupied and where the two police officers had just finished their search. They had found a good many items of clothing in the apartment, but nothing to indicate where he might have gone and certainly no newspapers. As he and the two men were leaving Madame Julie came out to see them.

'He has gone for good, has he not?' she said weeping. 'I shall never see him again, shall I?'

Gautier took the officers back with him to Sûreté headquarters in a fiacre. Madame Julie, they told him, was clearly bestotted with Marinetti but they had some sympathy for her. Her husband was a drunk who spent his evenings in cafés and bars, leaving her to run the building. As for Marinetti, they remarked with only a hint of envy, it was clear that no woman could resist him.

Next morning Gautier received another summons to the Director General's office. He found Courtrand pacing the floor of the room, a sign that at least a little of his vitality may have returned, although he still looked pale and drawn. He also had the look which Gautier knew well; the look of a man who had a secret of great importance, a part of which he was ready to reveal.

'I have asked you here, Gautier,' he said, 'because you should be present at a meeting which will shortly take place in this room.

Before that happens, I must make it clear that you will tell no one of the meeting, nor mention to anyone the name of the very important person who will be joining us presently.'

'I understand, Monsieur.'

'The person has come here at his own request.'

'Do you know the purpose of his visit?'

'Officially no, but based on my confidential knowledge of what transpires in the highest circles of the land, I believe I can make a shrewd guess.' Courtrand did not look at Gautier as he was speaking, a sure sign that he was bluffing and had not the faintest idea of why the meeting had been arranged. 'I may as well tell you now the name of the person who has asked for the meeting, but I repeat you must keep the information to yourself. It is no less a person than the Minister for War who will be joining us.'

Gautier had never met Ferdinand Gilles, who had taken up the appointment of Minister for War only a few months previously. He had the reputation of being a genial, popular politician, although some people doubted whether he had the the strength of purpose that would be needed in the post if there were to be a dramatic deterioration in the fragile balance of power in Europe.

'No doubt the Minister is going to ask us to have an officer appointed to keep a protective eye on his wife.' Courtrand was thinking aloud now. 'He is completely besotted with that wife of his you know.'

Gautier knew that Gilles had married relatively late in life and his bride had been some years younger than himself. 'Do they have any children?' he asked.

'None. That may explain why he is so protective towards her. Never trust a man who has no children, Gautier. He will always lack judgement.'

Gautier wanted to laugh. Courtrand was impossible. Not only must he have known that Gautier had never had a child, but he and his wife had also never had children. He was saved from having to make any comment for at that moment the Minister for War was shown into the room. Gilles was not an imposing figure and one could see at once that he was worried, for anxiety was etched into his expression. Even so he was able to contain it.

'And you must be the Director General's right-hand man,' he said to Gautier as they shook hands. 'Like everyone I have heard of your ability. I shall be relying on you in this difficult business.'

Gautier was drawn to the man. For a government minister to shake hands with a police officer and to show he had taken an interest in his work, was exceptional. 'I am at your disposal, Monsieur le Ministre,' he said. 'You can count on that.'

Gilles looked towards Courtrand and hesitated briefly. 'I may as well come to the reason why I am here, gentlemen,' he said. 'I have to tell you that my wife has been abducted.'

Gautier stared at him, reluctant to believe what he had heard. Not many days ago the British Ambassador had come into Courtrand's office and made a similar announcement about his daughter. One might have thought that this second announcement might be an elaborate joke, but government ministers seldom joked. Courtrand too was incredulous.

'Are you sure Monsieur? Could you not be mistaken?'

'She was out yesterday afternoon, attending a charity bazaar. In the evening when she did not return I assumed she had gone to spend the night with her sister, but when I telephoned her sister this morning I was told she had not been there.'

'Could your wife not have gone to spend the night somewhere else? With friends perhaps?'

'No, not possibly.'

Gautier realized that they were not being told the whole truth. The word 'abduction' implied if not kidnap, then at least being taken away against one's will. Was it possible that Gilles had used the word, as Sir Donald Macnab had, to conceal the fact that his wife had left him because she wished to? He could think of one question he might ask which would immediately provide the answer. Had Madame Gilles taken any of her clothes with her? If not then she may well have been taken away against her will. If she had taken clothes with her it was safe to assume she had left her husband because she wished to. Asking the Minister that question though might be seen as in a way challenging what he had told them. He was spared having to decide what to do, as Courtrand had questions of his own to ask.

'Do you know who spent the afternoon with your wife, Minister? Have you spoken with them? Have they any idea where she might have been taken? Have your servants seen any dubious characters hanging around your home during the last few days? Do you have any known enemies? Do you expect any demands for money to secure her release? Could you give us a detailed description of Madame, for I have not seen her myself recently?'

It was Courtrand's last question which gave Gautier an opportunity to ask his own. 'It would be helpful, Monsieur le Ministre, if we could know what she was wearing when you last saw her?'

The embarrassment of Gilles, which had clearly been growing with every question that Courtrand asked, now collapsed into a shameful denial. He had not actually seen his wife that afternoon, nor even in the morning for he had already gone to the Ministry when she must have left home. He fell back on bluster.

'I can only repeat, gentlemen, what I have already made plain. No one must know that I have come to see you this morning.'

'You have my assurances on that, Monsieur le Ministre,' Courtrand said.

'There could well be international repercussions if this became known,' Gilles continued. 'As you know this comes at a time of extreme tension in Europe. I cannot allow anyone to learn of this

141

unfortunate mishap, not even my colleagues in the Government. I am confident that you will discover the explanation of my wife's disappearance and then all will be well.'

'Nothing of what you have told us,' Courtrand said, 'will ever pass beyond these doors.'

Gilles continued his bluster, using all the clichés and gestures of an impassioned politician and one had the impression that he was not far from tears. Gautier began to feel sorry for the man, trapped as he clearly was in an emotional situation which was beyond his control. Eventually, after more protests and warnings he left, without giving any indication of what action he expected the Sûreté to take. Gautier said very little. He remembered how indignant Courtrand had been when he had doubted Sir Donald Macnab's claim that his daughter had been abducted.

When he and Courtrand were alone he felt he could at least ask a question. 'As I am sure you will agree, Monsieur, the Minister's visit has placed us in a difficult situation. What do you believe that we should do now?'

'Do?' Courtrand replied shouting angrily. 'Nothing!'

Back in his own office Gautier decided that it was not Courtrand's final remark which was surprising, but the belligerence with which he had made it. Even so, the Director General was right. By his insistence on silence, the Minister for War had effectively tied their hands. They could not put in train any of the usual enquiries which would help them trace his wife. No one in the Sûreté should be told what had happened. Until Gilles was ready to say more about his wife's disappearance nothing practical could be done.

Gautier put the whole incident out of his mind and began tackling other routine work. That afternoon there would be horse racing at Longchamps which would mean an influx of English visitors, who always enjoyed coming to Paris for the races. On the whole, English racegoers were well behaved and any trouble that might arise would be relatively minor as confidence tricksters, thieves and pickpockets tried to take advantage of their presence in the capital. Gautier did not anticipate any serious disturbances, but he arranged for a few precautionary measures to be taken.

As he thought of racing, he found himself wondering whether Rodier would be at Longchamps. Going racing, he had been told by his friend Nogaret, was one of the ways which Rodier used to project his image as a man about town. One might suppose that his duties were not so onerous that he could not find the time to spend an afternoon at Longchamps.

Gautier was still puzzled by the relationship between Edgar Wright and Rodier. Wright was a skilful and apparently successful businessman. From what Gautier had seen, he was clever and unscrupulous, ready at every opportunity to use people and manipulate them. One found it hard to see though what use he could make of Rodier, who would have no influence in the affairs of the country.

He was still thinking of Rodier when a messenger came up his office with a *petit bleu*. He guessed at once that it must be from Sylvie Lambert and he was right. The message read: I am giving a small dinner party tonight in my apartment at eight. Could you possibly come? I know this is absurdly short notice, but don't disappoint me. Not a second time!'

Sylvie had been right when she had said her dinner party was small. When Gautier arrived at her apartment that evening, he found that beside himself there were to be only two other guests, a married couple named John and Charlotte Prynne. Gautier saw them look at each other and smile as he bent to kiss Sylvie's hand, so he was not surprised when he learnt that they were English.

143

This, he guessed, must be the first time that they had been in France. Sylvie confirmed this and told Gautier that they would be spending only a week in Paris before starting on a tour which would cover Rome, Florence, Venice, Vienna, Munich and Marienbad, with two days in Brussels before they returned to England.

Gautier had heard of wealthy English people who undertook a 'grand tour' of Europe and wondered whether Mr and Mrs Prynne were equipped linguistically to get the full benefit of such a journey. To test their knowledge he began to say a few words to them in French, but Sylvie interrupted him.

'As a courtesy to our guests, Jean-Paul, we will speak only English this evening.'

'But you know my English!' Gautier protested 'I am far from fluent.'

'You will be,' Sylvie said smiling. 'You will be one day I promise you!'

Gautier had been wondering why, and at such short notice, he had been invited to dinner with the English couple. It must be, he decided, that another of Sylvie's friends, a Frenchman fluent in English, having accepted the invitation had been obliged to withdraw at the last moment. Even though she had been working in England for some years, Sylvie must have male friends in France, some in the diplomatic corps no doubt. If that were the truth, he had no objection to being at the dinner party as a substitute.

Their meal was served in the dining room of the apartment by a young French girl who also spoke fluent English. For most of the meal they talked of the journey on which the Prynnes were embarking. They had prepared diligently for their tour, reading the works of authors who had written about the places they were to visit. John Prynne had a prodigious memory and quoted whole

144

passages of Ruskin's work on Venice. Some might have found his recitations tedious, but Gautier listened intently, aware that by doing so he could learn about cities and paintings and sculptures which he knew he would never see himself.

Towards the end of the meal Sylvie took advantage of a break in the conversation to introduce another topic. 'Did you know,' she asked Gautier, 'that Mr Prynne is a friend of Edgar Wright?'

'Hardly a friend!' Prynne protested. 'I know he went to the same public school as me but I have never liked the man.'

'He has been very successful in his career, has he not?' Sylvie asked.

'But what a career,' Charlotte Prynne said disdainfully, 'selling the instruments of war!'

'Wright is in Paris on his own,' Gautier said. 'Did he never marry?'

He was curious to see whether Prynne would confirm what Surat had claimed, that Wright was a *pédé*. He had heard that sexual relations between men was not a subject which well-brought-up English people would ever mention in conversation, even though homosexuality was supposed to be rife in their country. So he had phrased his question in a way that would save Prynne from having to commit himself in his reply.

'I understand that he has the reputation of being a homosexual,' Sylvie said. She apparently had no inhibitions to restrain her.

'I wouldn't know,' Prynne said shortly, 'but he certainly was not one at school. If he had been he would have been expelled.'

Prynne's remark and the tone made it clear that he had no wish to talk about Edgar Wright, and for the rest of the evening Sylvie and Gautier had to listen to more talk about the Prynne's tour. Eventually even Gautier found himself growing weary of hearing about John Prynne's second-hand appreciation of Europe's art treasures, and it came as a relief when after dinner he and his wife said they must leave. They would be leaving their hotel early the following morning, they said, on a one-day visit to Versailles.

Gautier did not leave with them, for he had no wish to hear more about Ruskin in a fiacre driving back to the centre of Paris. In any case he sensed that Sylvie did not want him to leave and it was still relatively early. Back in the drawing room she poured him a glass of a fine old cognac and one for herself as they sat down to talk. Cognac was a man's drink in France and, Gautier had always heard, in England too, but he enjoyed seeing Sylvie cradling her glass in her hand and nosing the bouquet of the brandy. He was beginning to see that she was an unusual girl. He also knew she was unmarried and wondered why, supposing perhaps that like Ingrid she may have been divorced.

As they were sitting and drinking, Sylvie suddenly said to him, 'I am sorry for my little *bêtise*.'

'What *bêtise*?'

'I should never have mentioned that Edgar Wright had the reputation of being a *pédé*. Once they heard that, the Prynnes dried up and would say nothing about him.'

'Did you expect that they would?'

'I hoped that they might. After all that was my sole reason for inviting them to dinner. You told me you wished to find out more about him.'

Gautier tried to conceal his surprise. Sylvie had been more than helpful to him in London, arranging that he could meet Philippe Crespelle and then making all the arrangements for his journey to Scotland, but he had not intended to impose on her for assistance in his work in Paris. He told her as much.

Sylvie laughed. 'Why not? I believe we would make rather a good team, Jean-Paul. Tell me, what secrets of Parisians would you like me to uncover for you?'

Gautier laughed and they began to talk not of crime and criminals, but of life in Paris, of the Comédie-Française, of l'Opera, of the forthcoming Salon. Although Sylvie had a far greater knowledge of culture and current trends in entertainment than he had, Gautier felt that on the whole their views and tastes were not dissimilar. While they were talking, he suddenly thought of a question he might ask her and in which her opinion might help him. By asking it he would in effect be ignoring the insistence of the Minister for War that no one should be told of his wife's disappearance, but he had already decided that the Minister's request would be impossible to meet if the Sûreté were ever to trace his wife.

The question he asked Sylvie was oblique. 'Do you happen to know anything about the Minister for War?'

'Ferdinand Gilles? A little, although I have never had anything to do with him at a personal level. A charming man.'

'People seem to think he is not robust enough for a Minister for War.'

'I do not agree. In the current international situation the last person we want as Minister is a moustachioed, sabre-rattler. I believe he was appointed simply because he is a reasonable man. The Government hopes that he will be able to take the strain out of our relations with Germany, that he will work for compromise rather than confrontation.'

'Do you know his wife?'

Sylvie paused before she answered. Her pause could have been interpreted in different ways: hesitation because she did not know how to reply; a civil servant's natural caution; the time she needed to phrase an answer which would tell no more than the bare truth. Eventually she said, 'I have met her once, that is all.'

'And what impression did you form of her,' Gautier said, and then he added, 'you can tell me in confidence, Sylvie. In fact I would like you to treat our whole conversation in the greatest confidence for reasons which I may be able to explain one day.'

'I will give you an answer, Jean-Paul, but not this evening. Let's talk again in a day or two.'

11

Next morning as he was walking from his home to the Sûreté, Gautier stopped for a few minutes on Pont Royal. He had no reason for stopping, but for more years than he cared to remember on his way to work at the start of the day he had followed the same routine, leaning over the parapet of the bridge and looking at the river. For him the Seine was the embodiment of Paris, carrying with its slow-moving grace so much history, so many secrets.

That morning though he was thinking not of history nor of secrets, but of Sylvie Lambert. She had come back into his life, only briefly because in time she would be posted to another diplomatic mission and leave Paris, but in the meantime he would be able to enjoy her company. She might also be able to help him in his work and had already made it plain that she would be willing to do so. One of the difficulties he had always faced was that he had no one with a knowledge of the Government's current policies and strategies to whom he could turn for advice. By his self-seeking behaviour Courtrand had lost the confidence of all the senior people in the administration. Gautier did have access of a sort to the Prefect of Police, but that must be used sparingly and with caution. Sylvie, he was sure, had contacts at a high level in the Government and because she was agreeable and transparently honest people would confide in her. She would also be aware that Gautier would never impose on the friendship they had formed.

When he reached Sûreté headquarters he was told that someone had been trying to speak to him on the telephone. The caller had rung more than once, refusing to give his name or explain what he wanted. Only the Chief Inspector could help him. Gautier was mildly surprised. There were always cranks who tried to insist on speaking to him, but they seldom telephoned so early in the morning.

'If he calls again,' Gautier said, 'put him through to me.'

He had scarcely entered his office when the telephone rang. He did not recognize the voice of the man at the other end of the line, but there was no mistaking the urgency of his tone.

'Inspector Gautier? This is Beaumarchais.' At that point the name meant nothing to Gautier. He waited and the man added, 'From the Hôtel Londonderry.'

Immediately a minor alarm bell rang. The Londonderry was the hotel in which Fiona had taken her revenge on him. Then knowing Fiona, he decided that any trouble she may have caused at the hotel must be capable of an easy solution. She was a tiresome, petulant girl, but nothing more.

'What is the problem?' he asked Beaumarchais. 'The bill? If so leave it with me.'

Fiona had been staying at the Londonderry for some days. It would not be the first time that a hotel in Paris had been faced with bills incurred by the progeny of diplomats and other people in high places, but in these cases one had to deal with the problem quickly, efficiently and in a way which avoided scandal. The management of the major hotels understood this very well.

'It is not the bill, Inspector,' Beaumarchais replied, 'but something far more serious. It would be best if you came round to the hotel yourself and as quickly as possible.'

'If you insist, of course I will come,' Gautier said, 'but tell me at least what trouble I am to expect.'

'Monsieur,' Beaumarchais said softly, as though he were afraid of being overheard 'Mademoiselle Macnab is dead.'

Fiona's naked body lay stretched out on the carpet in the drawing room of the suite. One did not need medical knowledge to know how she had died. The grimace on her face and the distortion of her throat showed that she had been strangled, and the upper part of her body was disfigured by the bruises of a savage beating. Gautier had seen bodies as mutilated as hers before, but never in a first-class hotel and he was appalled by the viciousness of the attack on Fiona.

'Have you sent for a medical examiner?' he asked Beaumarchais.

'Not yet, Monsieur.'

'Why ever not?'

'We knew the mademoiselle was a friend of yours,' Beaumarchais said lamely.

Suddenly Gautier understood what the man was implying. The management must have known he had been entertained by Fiona in her suite. They may also have known or guessed at the sexual nature of what had occurred that evening. Now Beaumarchais must be wondering whether Gautier had paid a second visit to the suite and whether perhaps he had been carried away by a paroxysm of lust and had killed her.

'When did you find Mademoiselle Macnab's body? This morning?' he asked Beaumarchais.

'Yes, Monsieur. The maid found it when she came into the room to draw the curtains.'

'Was she seen in the hotel at all yesterday?'

'Yes, several times.'

'Then it seems likely, does it not, that she was murdered sometime yesterday evening?' Beaumarchais nodded so Gautier continued, 'I can tell you that last night I was dining with friends.'

'Inspector, I never thought for a moment. . . .' Beaumarchis left the sentence unfinished.

'And when was the last time Mademoiselle Macnab was seen alive?'

'She was in and out of the hotel often during the day and in the evening she dined in her suite.'

'Did she have a guest in the evening?'

'I am not sure, Monsieur.'

Gautier knew that Beaumarchais was being evasive. Any good hotel had ways of knowing if a guest entertained a visitor in her room, and even more so in a suite. A visitor might escape the vigilance of the desk clerk, but there would be other staff who would carry back intelligence to the management: chambermaids passing along the corridors, waiters carrying drinks. How else could Beaumarchais have known that he, Gautier, had been in Fiona's suite late at night? There would be ways later of finding out why Beaumarchais was being evasive, but in the meantime there were more important and urgent duties to which the police must attend. The first and most important action needed to make up for the delay caused by Beaumarchais's well-meaning endeavours was to carry out the routine police procedures always carried out after the discovery of a dead body.

A medical examiner must be sent for to establish the cause of Fiona's death and the British Embassy must be told. Gautier debated how he should do this. Surely a simple telephone call would not be enough? And whomever he told would have the responsibility of informing Fiona's parents. Eventually, after a prolonged telephone call to the Embassy and using all the weight of his authority, he was allowed to speak to the most senior officer on duty and was able to persuade him that he must come to the Hôtel Londonderry without delay.

When the man, whose name was Gibson arrived, Gautier, who did not know his rank, was surprised to see how young he seemed to be. In spite of that he looked at Fiona's body without flinching and left at once, saying he must arrange for a signal to be sent to her parents in Britain. Gautier thought it sad that Sir Donald and Lady Macnab would only hear of the death of their daughter through an impersonal diplomatic 'signal', but he was not in a position to interfere and even if he could have, he would have not have cared to pass the news on to them personally.

When Gibson had left and the medical examiner had arrived he told Beaumarchais, 'Make me a list of all your hotel staff who were on duty at any time during the last twenty-four hours. I will arrange for two police inspectors to be here within an hour to interview each staff member separately. Please arrange that two rooms are put at their disposal for that purpose.'

As he walked back to Sûreté headquarters, Gautier knew that the horror he had felt when he first saw Fiona's body had abated and that what he felt for her now was pity, a pity which would only diminish with time. He remembered how on the cross channel steamer she had wanted to make love, how he had refused her and how in the Hôtel Londonderry she had taken her revenge. Was it possible that by his rebuff he had in some way intensified her desire for sex? He dismissed the thought as ludicrous. Fiona had become obsessed with sex. One could not say why; perhaps because she was not an attractive girl and had never married. Gautier remembered her father saying almost with a hint of contempt that his daughter had never had a romantic attachment in her life. One could see now that one of the reasons she had fled to Scotland with Kossuth had been to enjoy a romantic experience and no doubt, she hoped, sex.

Following that line of reasoning, one might wonder whether it

153

had been the fact that she had been left alone in Paris free of her 'jailers', free to live in a hotel and to behave how she liked which had triggered off her obsession. She had been staying at the Hôtel Londonderry for some nights before the soirée of the Duchesse de Nièvre and may well have used them to entertain other men in her suite. If that was the case, as Gautier had discovered, she had quickly learnt some of the finer points of physical seduction. The enquiries he had initiated at the hotel would reveal how many more men she had taken there on previous nights. He had to know how many and who they were as quickly as possible. However ludicrous it might seem, until Fiona's killer had been identified, rumours would spread, tongues would wag and he would remain under suspicion.

When he arrived back at the Sûreté he was told that the Director General's secretary had a message for him. Corbin was a tiny man who worked in a room not much larger than a broom cupboard which led off Courtrand's imposing office. No one could deny his efficiency and over the years he had accumulated a massive amount of confidential information on every aspect of the Sûreté's work, much of it on people and personalities who would have been devastated if they knew he possessed it. People said that if he were to turn to blackmail, no one in the Government, commerce or society would be safe.

'The Director General will not be in the office today,' he told Gautiet. 'He is indisposed.'

'I am not surprised,' Gautier replied 'He looked really ill when I saw him yesterday.'

'In his absence I have been asked to give you a message.'

'By whom?'

'I am not supposed to tell you.' Corbin grinned. As always his grin was malicious. 'In fact I am not meant to know from whom the mes-

154

sage came, to whom I was speaking. Can you believe that? But of course I do. The mysterious secret personage is the Minister for War.'

'And the message?'

'You are to go to the Cercle de la rue de Rivoli at one o'clock. When you arrive at the club simply give your name, not your rank and in no circumstances reveal that you are from the Sûreté. You will be taken to the anonymous person who wishes to see you there. I understand that you and this person will lunch together at the club.' Corbin grinned again. 'The Director General will be upset at missing a free lunch and especially one in such aristocratic surroundings.'

The Cercle de la rue de Rivoli was one of a small number of clubs which had been formed in Paris over the last two or three decades, modelled on the gentlemen's clubs of London. Although the French believed that their country was the cultural centre of the world and that no other nation could match its sophistication and elegance, its food, wine and fashion, Frenchmen could not help imitating the dress and habits of English gentlemen. Part of the blame for this might be laid on King Edward VII who, as Prince of Wales, was a frequent visitor to Paris, where he was immensely popular in society as well as in the Moulin Rouge, cafés and in *maisons de tolerance* or upper-class brothels.

The Cercle de la rue de Rivoli had a balcony on its first floor which overlooked the Jardin des Tuileries and where members met to exchange the latest international news or social gossip before taking their lunch. When he arrived at the club Gautier was taken by an attendant up to the balcony, but instead of stopping there they passed on to the dining room, where the Minister for War was waiting.

'How good of you to come,' Gilles said. 'I was sorry to hear that our friend Courtrand is unwell, but if anyone can help me I am sure it is you.' Gautier realized that anonymity was at all costs

155

to be preserved at their meeting and to confirm this Gilles said, lowering his voice, 'I thought that if you have no objection we would lunch immediately. Most members lunch much later and as you can see we can have a little privacy now.'

The dining room was empty apart from themselves and one or two hovering waiters, but Gilles waited until they had both placed their orders and been poured a glass of wine before asking the question he had been suppressing. 'You have had no news of my wife, I suppose?'

'No, Monsieur, I regret not. And you?'

'Nothing, which only confirms that she must have been abducted. Madame Gilles would never leave me to suffer like this. She would have sent me a least a word to say she was well.'

Gautier could not help thinking it odd that a man who obviously doted on his wife should refer to her by a title and not by her Christian name. Perhaps there were nuances in their relationship, which would only become apparent later and which might possibly be related to her disappearance.

From his pocket Gilles took a piece of paper which he handed to Gautier, circumspectly, as if to make sure that no one could see what he was doing. Glancing at it Gautier decided that it must be an article cut from a foreign newspaper, but if so it meant nothing to him. He looked at Gilles enquiringly.

'I do not know what the article is about,' Gilles said, 'or where it comes from, but I suspect that it is written in one of the Slav languages. I found it in my wife's boudoir.'

'Would your wife understand it?'

'Almost certainly, yes. She is an exceptionally gifted linguist; fluent in French, German and English – tri-lingual one might say. And as you know, linguists, with their knowledge of the origins of words and the construction of sentences, can grasp the meaning of anything written in virtually any language.'

He told Gautier that he had found the article between the pages of a book in his wife's boudoir. Then he added that since his wife had disappeared he had spent much of his time sitting in her boudoir, feeling in a way that she was still there, that he was still with her. Although he did not say so, he had clearly also been hunting in the room for anything which might explain her disappearance.

'May I keep the article?' Gautier asked.

'By all means, and have it translated if you feel it may help you to know where she has gone.'

Gautier put the article in his pocket. What Gilles had said was the nearest he had come to admitting that his wife may have left home of her own volition. Once again he could see resemblances between her disappearance and that of Fiona Macnab. He had the feeling that her sudden departure from home might well be a case not of *cherchez la femme*, but of finding, or at least identifying, the man.

They continued talking as they lunched, or it might be more accurate to say that the Minister for War did the talking and all of it about his wife. Gautier did not mind listening, for one learned more by listening than by talking and gradually he began to form a mental picture of Madame Gilles. She had clearly been spoilt, outrageously so, all her life and he knew that Parisians had considered her to be, if not beautiful, then at least most attractive. In the circles in which she and her husband moved she would receive all the attention and compliments that a vain woman would expect, but would attention be enough? Gautier knew that she was several years younger than her husband and he could not help wondering whether Gilles was giving her enough of the physical satisfactions which a healthy young woman would expect from marriage.

The dining room was beginning to fill up and as it did Gilles lowered his voice until one could scarcely hear what he was saying. One of a group of members who came into the room seemed vaguely familiar, but it was several seconds before Gautier recognized him as the man he had seen with Edgar Wright and Charles Rodier in the Café Corneille. It took him even longer to remember the man's name: François Dorval. While he and Gilles were still talking, Dorval came across the room towards them and from his attitude it was clear that he remembered Gautier.

As he was passing their table he said loudly, 'So I see we are now allowing policemen into our club. This really is too much!'

Gilles looked at him and seemed about to make some comment, but before he could do so, Dorval had passed and was out of earshot. The incident had clearly embarrassed Gilles and, wishing to reassure him, Gautier said, 'There is no way that he could have heard our conversation, Monsieur.'

'That is not what upsets me. That man's rudeness to a guest of mine was inexcusable. I shall take the matter up with the club's committee,' Gilles replied and then he added, 'You know him I suppose?'

'I have never spoken to him in my life and to the best of my knowledge I have only seen him once.'

'He is a particularly disagreeable young man. As far as I know his only claim to distinction is that he claims to be distantly related to a duke.'

'But he is a member of this club?'

'Yes, he has been for some time, but fortunately we have not seen him for some years. He left the club because it was said that he was going to live abroad, but mainly I suspect because he had not paid his dues. I am only surprised that he has been readmitted.'

'He is unpopular then?'

'Yes and deservedly so. I am told that in the past few days he has been bringing a guest here whom most of us would rather not have in the club.'

'Would that be Edgar Wright, the representative of the British armament company?' Gautier asked.

Gilles stared at him in surprise. 'How on earth did you know?'

Back in his office, reflecting on his lunch with the Minister for War, Gautier realized that he had learnt nothing that would help him trace Madame Gilles. All he had heard about her from her doting husband was praise. He had not even been told her Christian name. What he had learned was that Edgar Wright must clearly be using François Dorval as well as Charles Rodier to promote the business of his company. That was no reason for surprise, but he found himself wondering whether Gilles was cynical enough to realize what was happening and robust enough to resist Wright's manoeuvres.

Gautier liked Gilles, who had many of the qualities which he admired most in a man: kindness, tolerance and good manners. He suspected but did not know that Gilles was also honest. Honesty was a quality all too rare in politicians, but the man had integrity, one could be sure of that. Gautier had the feeling – it was no more than a presentiment – that the outcome of his wife's disappearance would be a disappointment to Gilles, and if so he hoped it would not be too crushing.

While he was still wondering how he could begin tackling the problem of Madame Gilles's disappearance, the reports of the two inspectors who had been interviewing the staff of the Hôtel Londonderry arrived. Their enquiries were continuing but they had established that Fiona Macnab had entertained a number of men in her suite during the time she had been staying at the hotel. At least one had been seen to arrive there every evening, some staying almost until dawn. Little attempt had been made to con-

ceal the visits nor the identities of the men, some of whom were
known to the hotel staff as men about town. One though was
known for another reason, as he was the coachman who drove
one of the carriages belonging to the British Embassy. On an earlier occasion there had been two visitors, one of whom had left
fairly early to be followed by another. Although this was not mentioned in the inspectors' reports, a simple calculation showed that
this must have been the evening when she had taken Gautier to
the hotel after the Duchesse de Nièvre's soirée.

The reports and the timing of his visit to the Hôtel
Londonderry meant that Gautier could no longer be suspected of
being involved in Fiona's death. Even so, reading them gave him
no satisfaction. Quite suddenly, and comparatively late in life, the
absence of her parents – her 'jailers' as she believed them to be –
seemed to have released in Fiona long repressed sexual frustra-
tions, which she had then been unable to contain and which had
ended with disastrous consequences. Gautier could only imagine
the anguish and incomprehension of her parents when they learnt
of her death. He himself could still see her bruised and mutilated
body and part of him still wondered whether, if he had been more
adroit in dealing with her importuning on the cross-channel
steamer, her death might have been avoided.

He put the thought out of his mind, because he knew that such
speculation would provide no answers, nor alleviate the pity
which he felt for Fiona. His efforts must be concentrated on dis-
covering who had killed her and making sure that he paid the
penalty for his crime. No sooner had he made this resolution
when a message arrived from Vienna which threatened to under-
mine it. The Austrian authorities now knew who had killed Igor
Andrassy. The murderer had himself been killed during a confrontation between the police and agitators protesting in favour
of the dissolution of the Austro-Hungarian Empire and the grant-

ing of freedom to the Slav nations. He was named as Walther Kossuth.

The news hit Gautier with a crushing impact. If Kossuth had killed Andrassy could that mean that he had also murdered Ingrid? He remembered the note which Andrassy had written to Ingrid, in which he had said that Kossuth was in Paris and suggested that they should meet to discuss this. At the time Gautier had wondered briefly whether Kossuth might have killed Ingrid and then dismissed the notion as absurd. Now the question had been thrown open again.

As there had been no signs of forcible entry, it had been assumed that Ingrid had admitted whomever had killed her into the apartment. Gautier had been unable to think of any circumstances in which she would have allowed Kossuth to visit her. Now he had to think again. Kossuth had been socially acceptable enough to be invited to a society ball and plausible enough to have persuaded an ambassador's daughter to elope with him across the channel and at her expense. Was it possible that Ingrid had been interested enough about his political activities to agree to interview him in her apartment? Gautier knew that Ingrid would have gone to some lengths to obtain a story which she could pass on to newspapers all over Europe as well as in the United States. Like all journalists, curiosity was a way of life for her.

Then Gautier remembered that Kossuth and Fiona had left for England together, but he was not absolutely sure on what day. It was possible that he had already left Paris when Ingrid was murdered. He quickly checked his records of Sir Donald Macnab's meeting with Courtrand and himself. They showed that Fiona and Kossuth had been seen boarding a train at the Gare du Nord on what must have been the morning of the day when Ingrid's body had been found. It was at least possible that he was leaving then to escape the consequences of his crime.

Soon after the first report another and more detailed one came in from Vienna. Kossuth had long been suspected of subversive activities and his passport had been confiscated some time previously, but that had not prevented him from slipping into France. With the support of dissident groups of Hungarian and Slav immigrants he had lived there for a time and had then moved to England, perhaps with a false passport, and now to Ireland. The passport requirements in Ireland were notoriously lax and from there he had been able to return to the Balkans. In Austria he had been exposed by a journalist, Igor Andrassy, whom he had shot and killed. Witnesses had seen the incident, so there could be no questioning Kossuth's guilt.

Gautier knew now that he would have to live with the possibility that Kossuth had killed Ingrid in her apartment. The painful memory of her naked body lying on the bed returned. He could not accept that she might have allowed Kossuth to sleep with her. A more plausible explanation was that when he had found out how much she knew of his activities, he had stabbed her, then stripped her body and tried to make it look as though she had been killed in a sexual frenzy. Side by side with that came another picture: that of Fiona's naked and battered body in the Hôtel Londonderry.

He knew that neither picture could ever be completely erased from his memory, but in the meantime he must concentrate on dealing with both murders. The fact that two women had been found dead in similar circumstances might be no more than a coincidence, but something else struck him as odd. First an ambassador and then a government minister had approached the police asking their help in the disappearance of members of their families. He asked himself whether this duality might be significant. Could it be a kind of real-life *double entendre*, with two meanings which he would have to understand before the whole truth could be comprehended?

Evening was approaching and he knew that he must soon go out and have a meal. He remembered the melancholy dinner he had eaten on the night after he had learned of Ingrid's death. On that occasion he had forced himself to eat in a café not far from her apartment in the Place des Vosges. This time he would go to Chez Piquet, which had happier memories. Recalling them, he decided on an impulse to improve his mood by sending a *petit bleu* to Sylvie Lambert. The message read: 'Would you by any chance be free to dine with me tomorrow night?'

12

The answer to his message came in a *petit bleu* which was brought into him at his office the following morning. It read: 'Of course I will. I was begining to think you would never ask!'

Gautier smiled. He could almost hear Sylvie laughing as she wrote her reply. He sent another message telling her that he would pick her up at her apartment at half past seven that evening and that in the meantime she could decide where she would like them to dine.

The exchange of messages lifted the lingering traces of the depression he had felt the previous evening and he turned his attention to the pile of reports which lay on his desk. One of the most interesting concerned Marinetti. At the journalists' office in Rue Réaumur he had posed as the correspondent of the *Corriere della Sera* as well as contributing to other Italian papers. It now appeared that the *Corriere* denied having any connection with him or having ever published anything he had written and so far no other Italian paper had been found that knew of him.

Marinetti had entered France legitimately and passport office records revealed that at various times, in addition to France, he had lived or travelled in several Balkan countries, Holland and Germany. The mention of Holland immediately sparked off the thought in Gautier's mind that he might have been in some way involved in Ingrid's death but he laughed it aside, telling himself that he was in danger of becoming paranoid. Enquiries into Marinetti's past and present whereabouts would continue, but he was not hopeful that they would learn anything pointing to criminal activities.

Meanwhile there was the question of Madame Gilles. After returning from his lunch at the Cercle de la rue de Rivoli he had sent the article which Gilles had given him to be translated and now both the original and the translation lay on his desk. Gautier could see nothing in them to say in what paper the article had been published, nor by whom it had been sent to Madame Gilles. The purpose of it seemed to be to call attention to the verses of a poet writing in the ancient Croatian town of Dubrovnik. Some of the poems, all of them on the theme of love, were quoted in the article. Even in translation one could see that they were highly sensual, calculated to arouse erotic feelings in the reader and in that sense almost pornographic.

Gautier knew nothing to suggest that Madame Gilles might have found the poems titillating. On the other hand both the article and the poems might well have interested her as a scholar and a linguist. One supposed that there were few poets of distinction to be found in Dubrovnik. It still worried him that he knew so little about her and without even a sketchy knowledge of her tastes and inclinations he could make no progress in finding where she had gone. Her name, age and other details would be available from public records, but her husband's insistence on secrecy prevented him from following even those basic lines of inquiry.

So he decided to put Madame Gilles on one side and to concentrate on the other papers which lay on his desk. Among them were the second reports of the inspectors who were investigating the death of Fiona Macnab. Based on their interviews with the hotel's staff, they were confident that they could identify most of the men whom the dead woman had entertained in her suite at the hotel, with the exception of the second visitor on the evening of her death. Even so it was still possible that he too could be identified. There were two members of staff who might well have seen and spoken to him, but whom the inspectors had not yet been able to interview: one a night porter who was at home sick and the other a chambermaid who had not reported for duty since the day of the murder, though no one knew why.

Gautier sent a message to the inspectors, urging them to complete their work as soon as possible and then he began dealing with the other more mundane reports on his desk. Most of them dealt with minor incidents and many involved American or English visitors at Longchamps races. A pickpocket had stolen the wallet of a man from Harrow and the purse of a lady from Weymouth, while an American had been unwise enough to place a substantial bet with a well-dressed Moroccan gentleman posing as a bookmaker whom he had never seen again. These incidents could easily have been dealt with by police officers in attendance at the racecourse but Courtrand, who had always admired the English, had made it a rule that all offences affecting the English, however trivial, should be reported to Chief Inspector Gautier. More recently the rule had been extended to embrace visitors from the United States.

Dealing with such incidents, even though they often required no more than delegating them to a junior officer, was time consuming and by the time his desk was clear, Gautier decided that it was late enough for him, without troubling his conscience, to go to the Café Corneille. Apart from reviving his appetite for lunch, visits to the café often gave him a useful insight into the current attitudes of the lawyers, writers and politicians who made up his group of friends there.

167

He was later than usual in arriving at the café and the conversation of the group was in full and slightly risqué swing. They
were discussing a dancer from Sumatra whose performances were
the talk of Paris, displaying as they did a suppleness in her body
with lascivious movements that seemed to deny not only the laws
of anatomy, but of gravity.

The bawdy wit of his friends amused Gautier, but did not completely efface the memory of the problems facing him. Taking
advantage of a pause in the banter, he said, 'Do you suppose that
we are to be interrupted today by a parade of the English arms
salesman and his retinue as we were the last time I was here?'

'Monsieur Edgar Wright? I would hardly think so,' Duthrey
replied. 'He will be fifty kilometres from here demonstrating a
new field gun which his company is hoping to sell to our army.'

They began discussing the new gun, which according to the
press was claimed to have not only a far higher rate of fire than
comparable field guns, but its shells were also supposed to have a
much higher penetration than those of other guns.

'Will the Minister for War be at the trials?' Gautier asked. He
had not heard of the trials of the new gun.

'Certainly,' Duthrey replied. 'The Ministry has already put out
a press statement to that effect.'

'And will anyone be accompanying Wright?'

'Technicians of course. And Charles Rodier according to the
statement.'

'So Rodier does still have political influence,' Gautier commented.

'Not a great deal,' the young lawyer said. 'Politicians are wary
of him after that indiscretion with the girl pupil.'

'That was years ago!' Froissart protested, 'and they say the girl
made all the running.'

'Even so.'

When he returned to Sûreté headquarters, Gautier was faced with two surprises. The first one was when he learnt that Courtrand was back in his office. Such seemed to be the state of the man's health that he had not expected seeing him back at work for weeks, even months. The second surprise was that everyone in the building appeared to believe that he, Gautier, had been suspended from duty and was required to report to the office of the Director General immediately. He was kept waiting for several minutes before he was admitted to Courtrand's office, a well-known device for increasing a culprit's anxiety.

'This time Gautier, you have gone too far!' Anger had brought a measure of vitality into Courtrand. 'You seem to believe that you can do as you please, ignore all rules and procedures, but I never thought that you thought yourself to be above the law. This time you will pay!'

'Monsieur?'

'You were supposed to be watching over that poor girl. You were in a position of trust. Now I am told you raped and murdered her! This will be the end of you, Gautier, the end of your career, disgrace and prison I have no doubt.'

Courtrand's temper had always been volatile and everyone in the Sûreté had faced his occasional bursts of rage and loss of control. In the normal way one knew that one must be patient and wait for the storms to blow themselves out. This time Gautier sensed that patience would not be enough. He was beginning to understand what had happened and knew he must take control of the situation.

'Am I to understand, Monsieur, that I am being accused of murdering Mademoiselle Macnab?'

'How could you have done it, Gautier? Do you imagine that you, who are meant to uphold the law, can ignore it?'

Courtrand had been pacing up and down the room as he always did when in a rage. Instead of replying to his question Gautier walked over to the desk. There, neatly arranged by Corbin, were folders in which lay all the reports awaiting the attention of the Director General. Among them, still undisturbed and unread, was a summary of the reports on the investigations which had been carried out into the death of Fiona Macnab.

Gautier picked up the folder and held it out to Courtrand. 'I take it, Monsieur, that you have not read these reports on the murder of Mademoiselle Macnab?'

'Of course I have read them. But they change nothing.'

'In that case you will know that Mademoiselle Macnab entertained a number of men in her suite at the Hôtel Londonderry and that we are very close to establishing the name of the man who killed her.'

'Are you saying that you did not go to her hotel?'

'Monsieur, you know that I escorted her back to her hotel after the Duchesse de Nièvre's soirée. Do you not remember commenting on that?'

'Gautier, I cannot be expected to remember everything you tell me. In fact I now cannot even believe anything you tell me.'

'You may like to know, Monsieur, that on the night when Mademoiselle was murdered I was dining with friends.'

'Then how can you explain that I have been assured by a person of the highest standing that if you were not yourself in charge of the investigation, you would already have been charged with the murder?'

'When was this accusation made?'

'Only an hour or so ago.'

'And who was this person who made it?'

'I refuse to tell you.'

'In that case I have no alternative but to refer this matter to a higher authority.'

Gautier was using an old strategy, bluff on bluff and it worked. Courtrand continued to protest and bluster. He had been given the information in confidence. How would the police ever be able to count on informers if they gave their names away? Finally he gave out the name, but reluctantly.

'I was told all this by a man of integrity and influence, a government servant, a Monsieur Charles Rodier.'

That evening Sylvie Lambert and Gautier dined at Chez Piquet. Sylvie had chosen the restaurant without giving any special reason for her choice, beyond saying that she had enjoyed the previous evening which they had spent there. Gautier wondered whether another reason may have been that she preferred to spare him the expense of taking her to one of the grander restaurants of Paris: Le Grand Vefour, Laserre or Laperouse. With her elegance and style she would be at home in any of these. It was only later when they had begun eating that she looked around her and explained her reason.

'What I really like about this place is the people who use it. I like their friendliness, the way they chat and make jokes and laugh across the tables.'

'Yes,' Gautier agreed, 'I know of no other restaurant quite like it.'

'Do you think that we could ever become part of the regular clientele?' Sylvie asked. 'As a couple I mean.'

'We would have to come here more often – regularly.'

'Well?'

Gautier smiled, but did not answer. Even though he was enjoying Sylvie's company, he was still conscious of the problems which had faced him through the day. What he found difficult to understand was why Rodier had come forward and accused him of murdering Fiona. Rodier, he had been told, was with Edgar Wright at

171

the trials of the new field gun. It was possible, one supposed, that he had not gone to the trials. One way of finding out would be to ask the Minister for War but that was not possible, at least for the time being.

Sylvie may have been aware that something was worrying him and presently she said, 'The last time we met you asked me if I knew anything about Madame Gilles.'

'The wife of the Minister for War? Yes.'

'I told you that I might be able to help you, but that first I had to be sure of my facts. In government service, as in every walk of life, one hears things, rumours speculation, gossip and very often what one hears can be misleading if not actually false. When Ferdinand Gilles married for the first time, which was not all that long ago, people working for the government were surprised. It did not seem a likely match.'

'For what reason?'

'As you know he is a good deal older than her, but on top of that she was thought to have a dubious past. Did you know that she had been married before?'

'And divorced?'

Sylvie smiled. Divorce carried a stigma in France and those who could afford one were never accepted in the upper echelons of society. 'Nothing as drastic as that! No, her first husband died, but while he was alive she was said to have led a rather lurid life.'

'In what way?'

'I really do not know, but apparently in those days she was known as Monsieur Nicolas.'

Monsieur Nicolas was a character in a book written more than a hundred years previously by Restif de la Bretonne and widely considered as an example of excessively sensual, if not erotic, behaviour.

'So she is felt to have enjoyed sex,' Gautier said.

'It is said so, though this was some years ago.'

'Was she not aware that the enjoyment of sex is the prerogative of men,' Gautier said lightly.

'Is it really? I wish someone had told me that when I was sixteen.'

They both laughed. Although he knew it was only a joke, Gautier found himself wondering about Sylvie's past. She must be thirty now and although not beautiful was attractive, elegant, amusing and with a bright, appealing personality. Yet she was not married and as far as he knew never had been, but she must have had and still have her admirers. He was still thinking about this when she asked him a question which, he supposed, he would have preferred her not to ask.

'Jean-Paul, what happened to the girl whom you brought back from Scotland?'

'She is dead. She was murdered.'

'Murdered! By whom?'

'We do not know yet,' Gautier replied and then on a sudden impulse he added, 'I may have been partly responsible for her death.'

Sylvie looked at him but said nothing. Gautier knew then that he must tell her everything. 'I will start at the beginning.'

He did start at the beginning of his relationship with Fiona, explaining to her how her father had come to the Sûreté and how he Gautier had been sent to Scotland to bring her home. He told Sylvie of Sir Donald's contemptuous dismissal of Fiona's romantic experiences and of how, once in Scotland, Fiona had been abandoned by Walther Kossuth. He described their journey back to France and how she had tried to seduce him in the cabin of the cross-channel steamer. He supposed that Sylvie might think he was making excuses for his subsequent behaviour, but that was not his intention, only to present the facts. Sylvie had always been transparently honest with him and he must be honest with her.

173

His accounts of their meeting at her home in Paris and at the
soirée of the Duchesse de Nièvre and his subsequent visit to the
Hôtel Londonderry were factual, bluntly so, for he had no wish
for them to be seen as a confession, even though he had not
entirely freed himself of a feeling of guilt. If Sylvie were shocked
it was no more than he deserved. She listened without showing
any signs of emotion. Then when he had finished she reached out
over the table and placed her hand on his.

'*Mon chou*,' she said softly, 'do not allow what happened to
upset you. It could have happened to any man.'

When Gautier left Sylvie outside her apartment she did not invite
him in for a glass of cognac, saying that she was leaving Paris the
next morning and had to make an early start. At first Gautier supposed this might mean that she had been given another posting,
which would mean another two or three years away. He did not
have to ask her, for she then told him that she was going to see
her parents in the Dordogne but for only two days. She also
added that her father was a farmer.

'Ours is only an ordinary bourgeois farm,' she added, 'not one
of these great landed estates.'

Gautier was relieved to hear that she was from a family of modest background. With her manner, appearance and professional
standing she might be thought to belong at a higher social level.
At the same time he wondered why he was concerned about her
upbringing. Did that mean that their relationship was developing
in new directions and if so was this what he wanted?

'I would like to meet your parents one day,' he said cautiously.

She placed her hands on his shoulders and kissed him on the
lips, smiling. 'Oh, you will Jean-Paul,' she said, 'I can promise you
that you will.'

As the fiacre which he had kept waiting was driving him into the centre of Paris, he decided it was too early for him to return home. The ghost of the guilt he had felt over Fiona's death had been exorcized, but it had been replaced by another, a feeling that instead of enjoying the evening he should have been engrossed in solving the murder of Ingrid, as well as the two other murders still unsolved in the files of the Sûreté. So he allowed himself to be driven to Quai des Orfèvres.

On his desk the reports of the day's crimes were accumulating. At that point only those committed during the previous night and early that morning would be included and there would be plenty more to come. Compared with the relatively minor offences in which English and American visitors were involved and which came to him all too frequently, they made grisly reading. The home of a moneylender had been stripped after he, his wife and two children had been stabbed to death; a vendetta between rival gangs of ruffians had erupted in the early hours into a fight with knives and razors on Boulevard Saint-Denis and four corpses had been taken to the mortuary; a girl aged no more than twelve had been found dead, raped and strangled, in the Bois de Boulogne, not far from the famous restaurant Le Pré Catalan.

A less grisly and less spectacular murder caught his eye among the list. A hotel not far from the Gare du Nord reported that a woman had been found dead in one of its rooms. Gautier knew that the hotel was one of several in a disreputable area used by prostitutes and their customers – *hôtels de rendez-vous* was how they were sometimes described. The woman had been taken there the previous evening by a man who had paid for the room and it was only in the morning that the woman had been found in it, on her own and dead.

On the surface there appeared to be nothing in the account of the murder to arouse interest or even curiosity, but Gautier's eye was caught by one word. The police officer who had written it had used the word *bossue* when describing the dead woman. Most people would think it strange that any man would have taken a hunchback to a *hôtel de rendez-vous*. Then Gautier suddenly remembered that when he had gone with Fiona to the Hôtel Londonderry they had been met at her suite by a chambermaid who, while not a hunchback, walked with a stoop, her shoulders well forward. He also remembered that a member of the hotel's staff, a chambermaid, was missing and no one knew why.

13

Early next morning Gautier came out of the mortuary to which the body of the woman found dead at the *hôtel de rendez-vouz* had been taken. He had recognized the woman and she was, as he had feared, the hunched chambermaid from the Hôtel Londonderry. He had sent instructions to the hotel that someone should go to the mortuary to make an official identification of the body, but he was certain it was that of the woman whom he had seen on the evening when he had arrived with Fiona at the hotel. Her name he was told was Martha. Now walking from the mortuary to the hotel itself, he felt an immense pity for her. She had been caught up in a murder or perhaps a series of murders for which she was wholly blameless.

Lonely, unloved, she would have found it hard to resist a man who had invited her to spend a night of passion with him in a hotel. She may probably never have heard of a *hôtel de rendez-vous*, nor of the sordid trade on which establishments like that thrived. Gautier wondered whether her killer might even have taken her out to dinner first, plying her with wine to break down any scruples or defences she might have had. This was just speculation, but the only plausible reason for murdering Martha must have been that she had seen the man whom Fiona had taken to her suite on the night when she had been murdered, and that she would have then been able to identify him.

The owner of the hotel, an Algerian named Mustapha, was not pleased to see him. He would have been expecting a second visit from the police, but might have hoped that it would not have been made by a Chief Inspector. He received Gautier with surly reluctance at the small reception desk in the narrow hallway. Above on each of the four upper floors were the bedrooms, also small. Mustapha had obviously been working on the hotel's register and immediately thrust it in front of Gautier.

'Forget the paperwork,' Gautier told him, 'I have questions for you to answer.'

The report from the local police which Gautier had seen the previous evening had been thorough, surprisingly so, and he had a mind to commend the officer who had written it. Martha and the man accompanying her had arrived at the hotel not long before midnight. They had paid for the room which the man said they would need for the whole night and had gone directly upstairs, taking with them a bottle of wine which the night porter had sold them. When signing the register they had given their names as a Monsieur and Madame Bovary. The porter, also from Algeria, had never read Flaubert and had not questioned the names. No noises or disturbances had been heard coming from their room during the night, suggesting that the porter may have fallen asleep, and the woman had been found dead only when a maid had knocked on the door shortly after eight o'clock in the morning. No one could say at what time the man had left the hotel.

Gautier told Mustapha that the police had established the identity of the woman and now he wanted to know more about the man. Little by little he extracted some meagre information from him and from the porter and the maid, who had also been brought in for the interrogation. The man, they said, was of medium height, well built and well dressed. No one of the staff knew anything about French regional accents and all they could say was

178

that the man was not from Algeria, nor any other part of Africa. The maid who had seen him only once passing on the stairs, volunteered the information that he was good-looking, far too handsome for the woman he had with him and suggested that he might have Latin blood. All three of them said they were surprised that a man of his appearance and style – a man about town, as they described him – would have wished to have sex with a woman who, while not totally unattractive, was clearly not a *putain* and did not appear to have much sexual appeal. When they arrived at the hotel, the woman had seemed excited and a little tipsy, nothing more. Deciding that he would learn nothing more from them, Gautier left the hotel, saying that he would send policemen to search the room in which the murder had taken place thoroughly and that in the meantime it should be sealed.

As he walked back into the centre of Paris he found himself thinking of Marinetti. He had not taken the hotel maid's suggestion that the murderer might have Latin blood seriously. After all she herself was from the Cote d'Azur and might by her colouring be mistaken for an Italian. He did not believe for a moment that Marinetti might have murdered Martha, but the man was missing and it was reasonable to assume that somewhere he might fit into the complex pattern of murders which the Sûreté had to investigate. Although he was reluctant to admit it, if Marinetti were to be suspected of a murder it would be more logical to link him with that of Ingrid. Even if his claim to be a journalist proved fraudulent, they had been colleagues at least on paper and he might have found a way to trick Ingrid into inviting him to her apartment on the evening she was killed. He was not only an attractive man, but plausible as well. However if that line were to be followed one had to think of a motive other than a sexual one. Gautier decided that he should not torture himself with that kind of speculation.

In his office at Sûreté headquarters Gautier found a letter waiting for him. Handwritten on pale blue notepaper, he saw with surprise that it was from Mrs Charlotte Prynne, who with her husband had dined with Sylvie Lambert and him in Sylvie's apartment. The letter began by saying how much Mrs Prynne and her husband had enjoyed meeting the Inspector over dinner and looked forward to seeing him again when they were next in France. Beyond that Mrs Prynne enthused about Paris, its historical splendour, the culture and courtesy of its people. Gautier recognized that the letter was no more than a convention; the good manners of the middle-class English, covering only one page and its reverse. No Frenchwoman would have written such a letter, or if she had it would have run to several pages. The letter ended with the usual expressions of sincerity and was signed 'Lottie Prynne'.

It was the word 'Lottie' which caught Gautier's attention. He remembered his friend Nogaret telling him that the girl pupil at the École des Beaux Arts who had been seduced by Rodier had been named 'Lottie'. Nogaret had not been sure about the girl's name, but had believed that it was of German origin. Now it seemed possible that spelt slightly differently it might be an abbreviation of Charlotte, a popular English name. In either case if the girl had been English and not German, that might throw some light on Rodier's otherwise odd relationship with Edgar Wright.

Anxious to know the truth, Gautier set out for the Bibliothèque Nationale. As all Frenchmen knew, the Bibliothèque was the repository of all literary knowledge and there he would surely find the answer to his problem. When he arrived there and explained his requirements a librarian had an instant answer. He must speak to Professeur Jean Cousin, an acknowledged authority on semantics, who had made a hobby of names and their meanings.

He found the professor in a tiny room whose walls were lined with books, while more books lay in untidy heaps all over the floor. Cousin was himself equally untidy, with long, straggling hair and a white beard. His eyes though were perceptive and full of humour. He found a chair for Gautier by pushing a pile of books off it on to the floor. After apologizing for what must seem to a professor to be a trivial matter, Gautier explained what he wished to know.

'I believe I can help you, Monsieur,' Cousin said. 'In principle your problem is not as simple to resolve as many might think. One must clearly take into account the spelling of the names, but there are other considerations; how they are pronounced, for example.'

'Really?'

'Oh yes. Pronunciation, accents, intonations can tell one so much about an individual: where he was born, for example and his upbringing. Take you, Chief Inspector. I would say that your family came from south-west France, but one of our parents, your mother no doubt, came from further north, Caen perhaps.'

Gautier was amazed. What Cousin was saying was true. He made a mental note that he should consult the Professor more often. He could think of a number of criminal cases in which his advice might have speeded up investigations. Cousin laughed, amused by his amazement. His laugh, a falsetto giggle, fitted in with the man's character without in any way detracting from his enormous erudition.

'In the matter I have in mind, Monsieur le Professeur,' Gautier said, 'the case dates back several years.'

'And you were not around at the time? Then you did right to

come to an old man like me.' Gautier was about to give some assurance that he did not believe Cousin was so old, when he realized that the Professor was still laughing at him. 'Am I right in thinking that you are talking of the Lottie who was a pupil at the École des Beaux Arts.'

'I am, Monsieur le Professeur.'

'The young lady who spent too long in the *garçonnière* of one of the officials at the *école*?'

Since Cousin evidently knew about the cause célèbre, Gautier could see no point in secrecy. 'Yes. Charles Rodier.'

'And you wish to know whether her name signified that she was English rather than German, as everyone at that time assumed? Then I can reassure you. Lottie Schuman's father was German, and although they lived in Strasbourg, he came originally from Leipzig. But her mother was not German. She had Spanish blood in her which was why the girl had been christened Carlotta, hence the nickname Lottie.'

'You appear very confident about this.'

'I am, Chief Inspector. Only a few days ago I was asked to look into the matter and I examined all the notes I made at the time. You see someone else has been taking an interest in the Lottie affair.'

'May I ask who?'

'Certainly. He said he was an Austrian and gave the name of Andrassy, but that was a lie. Although he spoke good French I could tell by his accent that he was an Italian, from Milan I would say.'

That day Gautier took his lunchtime aperitif at a café which he scarcely knew and where he was confident he would not be known. The man he would be meeting would also, he hoped, not be known. Marc Aligotte was a civil servant in the Ministry for

War. In Gautier's view he was an excellent civil servant: honest conscientious and able; too able perhaps, for successive Ministers for War had made sure that he would not be promoted too high.

Gautier liked Aligotte and had looked forward to seeing him again, although he sensed that there would be a less enjoyable aspect to their meeting. Ingrid and Gautier had met him a year or two previously, during a grandiose event devised by the then Minister for War, General Lucien Saint-Exupéry Gaspard. The event, designed to be a homage to Napoleon, had ended with none of the acclaim which the Minister had expected, but had become involved in the aftermath of three murders. All that was history now, but Gautier had not met Aligotte since Ingrid's death and he knew he would have to face his protestations of shock, his questions and his expressions of sympathy. The worst of his own grief was beginning to recede and he had no wish to be reminded of it.

A meeting with Aligotte was the only way he could think of learning more about the current Minister for War, Gilles, and more importantly about his wife. Because of the conditions of secrecy which Gilles had imposed in the matter of his wife's disappearance, tact had been needed in arranging the meeting. Gautier had first established that Gilles would not be at the Ministry at the time and unlikely to be asking for Aligotte. Then he had let it be known that he was making confidential enquiries into the activities of the Englishman Edgar Wright. There was at least an element of truth in this and Gautier was certain that Aligotte would come to the meeting ready to be cooperative. In his experience, while *petits fonctionnaires* were habitually obstructive, senior civil servants did what they could to help each other and the police.

When they met in the Café Joubet and had ordered their aperitifs, mercifully for Gautier, Aligotte did not spend too long over his condolences, although there could be no doubting that they were genuine. After exchanging a few further courtesies, Gautier told him that the authorities were concerned about the activities of Edgar Wright. Of course there was no question of criminal charges, but he had been asked to keep a watchful eye on certain characters with whom Wright appeared to be friendly and who were not known for their integrity or even honesty. He learnt nothing from Aligotte which he did not already know, but gradually he was able to steer the conversation in the direction of the Minister for War.

'Your Minister,' he told Aligotte, 'has the support of everyone who cares about the future of France. The deal which he has done over the field guns should strengthen our military position enormously.'

'It will of course, although the purchase of the guns has not yet been ratified.'

'I thought it had been.'

'It will be, but the Minister is at this moment in meetings with the English suppliers, scrutinizing the contracts, studying the small print one might say. We have to be sure that the same guns are not being made available to other powers.'

'To the Germans? You sound as though you do not trust the English.'

'Who does? We are planning to buy more weapons from Lydon-Walters – a whole range of rifles, bayonets and small arms – but we have to be certain that the company is not supplying the same arms to the Germans.'

'Are you sure that the Minister can secure this deal?'

'Certainly. It may take a week or more to settle everything, but the Minister has the backing of the President and of all other Ministers involved, as well as, of course, that of his staff.'

'And his wife? Will she support him?'

Aligotte looked at Gautier quickly. 'Why do you ask that?'

'I understand that she is German by birth.'

'That is simply not true,' Aligotte said. 'Just because at one time her family lived in Strasbourg, people said she must be German. You have only to talk to her to realize she must be French.'

'So we can rely on her being by her husband's side in this difficult period?'

Aligotte's reaction showed Gautier that he had gone too far. The man knew something about the Minister's wife, but loyalty would prevent him disclosing it. All he said was, 'I understand Madame Gilles is out of Paris at the moment.'

Now, even though he was conscious that he had been maladroit in dealing with Aligotte and would learn no more from him, like a committed angler Gautier could not resist making one last random cast. 'Is it true that as a girl Madame Gilles studied at the École des Beaux Arts?'

'How would I know? She is a woman of almost forty, so if she did, that would have been more than twenty years ago.' Aligotte smiled. 'I know I look old for my age, but I was not in the service at that time.'

Later that afternoon Gautier told Surat about his meeting with Aligotte. His suggestion that Madame Carlotta Gilles had been the girl who had shared Rodier's *garçonnière* had been no more than a guess. He had no proof that Gilles's wife had been the Lottie who had caused the scandal which might have ruined Rodier at the École des Beaux Arts. Yet as he looked back at what little he had been told about Madame Gilles – her past reputation, the highly salacious verses she had been sent and even her husband's desperate craving for her to be returned to him – it all seemed to indicate that sex had always played a dominant part in her life.

185

'Mine may have been no more than a guess that she was the girl,' Gautier said, 'but it might have been an inspired guess. We will find out in due course no doubt.'

He told Surat as much as he needed to know about the disappearance of Madame Gilles, explaining that the matter was to be treated as highly confidential. No one was to be told, whether in the Sûreté or not, of any developments that might take place. He had given the Minister for War his word on that.

'Then how are we to trace her?' Surat asked.

'In my opinion she has been taken from their home, perhaps by force or possibly with her own agreement.'

'Like the British Ambassador's daughter?'

'One might put it that way. In either case her safety must be our main concern. Perhaps the best way of ensuring that might be to ignore her, to assume she is happy where she is and leave her there. In the meantime we can concentrate on the other characters in this melodrama.'

'Have you anyone in mind?'

'I am going to ask you to make another trip to the neighbourhood of Edgar Wright. Find out as much as you can about this man François Dorval. From what you told me he appears to be living in Wright's apartment. I have heard that Dorval left the country under financial difficulties and if Wright is now subsidizing him I would like to know why.'

'I will do my best, *patron*.'

After Surat had left, Gautier got out all the notes and other papers in his desk which dealt with the murders under investigation: that of Ingrid, of the Comte d'Artagnan, of Fiona Macnab and of Martha, the maid at the Hôtel Londonderry. At one time he had thought that the murders might be linked, moving in two parallel currents of crime. Now he had decided that any connection between them was more likely to be unplanned, explained by chance circumstances.

The first thing he should do was to examine the timing of the murders. Ingrid, he knew, had been killed on the evening before he had returned to Paris. On the following morning Fiona Macnab had left Paris with Walther Kossuth. The note which Andrassy had written to Ingrid made it clear that they both knew of Kossuth, and it was likely they believed that what they knew might provide material for a story in the press. Following this reasoning Gautier had at one time wondered whether Kossuth might have killed Ingrid to protect himself before fleeing to Scotland. Even though Kossuth had later killed Andrassy in Vienna and was himself now dead, he no longer believed that this could have been the case. Knowing his background, Ingrid would never have admitted Kossuth into her apartment and there had been no signs that he might have forced an entry.

Thinking of the timing of her death, he remembered that her concierge had found Ingrid's body at around midday when she had taken a packet which had arrived for her up to her apartment. Suddenly that posed more questions. What was that packet and what had become of it? He had seen no packet in her apartment that first evening. Was it possible that it might have some bearing on her murder?

Learning more about the packet proved more troublesome than one might have expected. At first the concierge denied any knowledge of it, or even that she had given its arrival as the reason why she had gone up to Ingrid's apartment and found her body. Gautier set Surat to work on her. Surat had a long experience of concierges and his own way of dealing with them. He knew their weaknesses. Many of them were too fond of drink, finding comfort in their long, lonely evenings from wine. Others were widows and more than once Surat had been obliged to endure the attentions of ageing ladies in order to extract information from them.

By employing one or other of his strategies, he managed eventually to persuade Ingrid's concierge to admit that a packet had
been delivered for her on the day of the murder. At first she
claimed to have no idea of what had happened to it. Then under
pressure she admitted that she had opened it and seeing that it
was of no value, thrown it away. All the packet contained, she
said, was newspapers; to be more precise two copies of some foreign newspaper.

'Did she say what country the paper came from, or in what language it was written?' Gautier asked Surat when he was reporting
on his meeting with the concierge.

'She has no idea. She is even less of a linguist that I am.'

'But can we assume that the paper was not from America?'

'I think that would be safe. I gave her a few words in different
foreign languages in the hope that she might recognize one of
them as being in the title of the paper, but it was hopeless.'

'As you know, Madame Van de Velde contributed to several
papers in different countries,' Gautier said. 'I would think that
this packet might well have contained copies of articles which she
had written and which were being sent to her as a courtesy.'

As he was speaking Gautier remembered the batch of articles
which Surat had found in a rubbish bin outside Ingrid's apartment. Her main interests in what she wrote were in political and
social issues and the articles had been written for papers in a number of countries apart from France and including Germany,
Austria, Holland and Italy. The fact that her murderer had thrown
her articles into the rubbish bin suggested that he may have
thought that they may possibly have contained something which
would have pointed to his identity. Gautier realized even so that
it would not be practical to show the concierge copies of all the
papers for which she had written, in the hope that she might recognize one. At one time he had suspected both Kossuth and

188

Andrassy as possible murderers, but both had been in effect eliminated and he would have to find others.

After Surat had left his office he glanced at *Le Figaro* which lay on his desk. A copy of the paper was delivered to him every day and when he had time he tried to read at least part of it, mainly through loyalty to his friend Duthrey, for in general he found its style of journalism a little too austere for his taste. One of the leading stories that day was the purchase by the French Government of field guns, rifles and other arms.

'The sale to the French Government not only of field guns but a whole range of arms,' the piece read, 'will be a great coup for Lydon-Walters, the English armaments company.'

It was the use of the word 'coup' which intrigued Gautier. He was aware of the common uses of the word in expressions like *coup de grâce*, *coup d'état* and even *coup de théâtre*, but in the context of the *Figaro* article, the word used on its own seemed to mean a master stroke executed with finesse and even an element of duplicity. He knew of course that this was his own interpretation, but at that moment he decided that he would solve the murders facing him with a single coup of his own.

14

Gautier knew that his coup would require not only careful planning, but the support of at least one senior figure in the Government. Since Courtrand was unlikely and perhaps physically unable to give him any practical assistance, the following morning he decided that he would go to the Préfecture de Police in the hope that, even though he had not made an appointment, he might be able to speak to the Prefect.

He was kept waiting at the Préfecture, but not for as long as he had expected.

The Prefect was an exceptionally busy man, largely because he took an interest in so many aspects of the administration of Paris, very often in matters which were of no real concern of his. Other senior officials seldom objected, partly because he had such an agreeable personality and partly because those indolent by nature were not sorry for his interference. When Gautier was admitted to his office, he looked at him expectantly.

'Well Gautier', he said, 'what news do you have of our Englishman's machinations?'

'Not as much as I had hoped, but Monsieur Wright has a tight ring of defence.'

'What do you mean?'

'He is a devious character and has recruited a small army of

lieutenants, all of them helping him, but none in ways that openly break the law.'

'Are you talking of Rodier?'

'Rodier is only one of them.'

'If all these men are above the law why did you come to see me
this morning?' the Prefect asked.

'I was hoping to have your support, Monsieur le Préfet, for a
plan which I hope will expose not only Wright but all his lieutenants.'

'Tell me about it.'

Gautier told him that what he had in mind was to bring together Edgar Wright and those who had been helping him on an occasion when they would all feel obliged to attend and which none
of them could possibly regard with suspicion. Senior government
officials would also be invited to lend the occasion an air of
authenticity.

'What I had in mind was a reception to celebrate the signing of
the arms contracts,' he explained. 'The Government would be the
hosts and the Minister for War would of course be present.'

'I am not sure,' the Prefect said 'that the signing of those contracts should be an occasion for celebration. Some people feel that
the terms agreed were too favourable to the English firm.'

'Perhaps the Minister was under unreasonable pressure to agree
to them.'

'Perhaps. Go on.'

'In that case, the celebration might give us a reason for rene-
gotiating them.'

The quick, questioning look which the Prefect gave Gautier
suggested that he might know, or at least suspect, to what pressure Gilles had been exposed during the negotiations over the
purchase of arms, but he said nothing. Instead he asked, 'Where
do you think this reception should be held?'

'Why not at Wright's apartment? I understand it is large enough.'

'I think that would be a mistake. I am not sure what you think may happen during the evening, but having it at his home would place Wright at an advantage. No, leave it to me and I will choose a suitable venue.'

'Then you will see that all the arrangements are made and the invitations sent out?'

'Not by me personally, but I am certain that the Ministry of War will be receptive to anything I suggest. Can you let me have the names of those who should be invited?'

'Not at the moment, Monsieur le Préfet, but very soon. There are certain carefully contrived situations which need to be put in place first.'

The Prefect smiled and shook his head. 'And you say that Edgar Wright is devious!'

If his coup was to succeed Gautier knew that he would need an element of good fortune in any circumstances which might arise outside his direct control. The first such stroke of luck came sooner than he might have expected. When he arrived back at the Sûreté he was told that a woman was waiting there and insisted on seeing him. The woman proved to be the concierge of the building in which Ingrid had lived. Gautier was told that the concierge had come to see Surat, but as Surat was not there she was demanding to be taken to Gautier. No amount of persuasion would make her agree to leave until she had spoken to the Chief Inspector.

Madame Vize might be considered the archetypal French concierge. Her appearance, dress, and manner resembled those of scores of concierges. If she differed from others it might be in her probity, or lack of it, her capacity for finding excuses for deviant

193

behaviour and her unshakeable belief that life had treated her harshly, but Gautier knew he was not obliged to judge her in such matters. He accorded her the same courtesy as he did all women.

When she was seated in the chair opposite his own he asked her, 'Madame, how can I help you?'

'It is your colleague whom I wish to see. Are you sure he will not mind my talking to you?'

'You may not remember me, Madame, but I was the friend of Mademoiselle Van de Velde who came to her apartment on the afternoon after she was murdered.' Madame Vize gasped and clapped her hand over her mouth. '*Mon Dieu*! Of course! How could I forget you and that dreadful afternoon?' The enormity of her gaffe and the memory of Ingrid's murder overwhelmed her and she began to cry, tears coursing slowly down her cheeks.

Gautier passed her his handkerchief. 'Do not upset yourself, Madame. Anyone could be excused for not remembering me. At that time I was not a policeman, but a grieving suitor.'

His remark did little to staunch Madame Vize's tears, but after a time she was ready to say why she had come to the Sûreté that morning. Surat, she explained, had questioned her repeatedly and sternly about the packet which had arrived for Mademoiselle Van de Velde on the morning after her murder and which, as she eventually remembered, she had thrown away. All she had been able to tell Surat was that the packet had contained two copies of a newspaper, a paper in a foreign language which she could not understand. She could not even tell him the name of the paper.

'It was only later,' she told Gautier, 'only last night in fact that I remembered something about the title of the paper.'

'And what was that?'

'I may not understand foreign languages, Monsieur, but I do know how to spell. The title of that paper had been wrongly spelt.'

'In what way?'

'They had spelt the name "Sarah" as "Sera". I should know because my daughter's niece was christened "Sarah". People used to laugh at us, saying that it was an affectation, but the sister of my daughter's husband chose the name in honour of Sarah Bernhardt the actress. Fancy anyone not knowing how to spell her name!'

As he heard the concierge spell the two names out, Gautier's brain raced ahead. He let her finish what she had to say, not yet ready to believe that she may have given him a clue to the identity of Ingrid's murderer. He waited patiently until she had told him how her daughter had once seen the great Sarah Bernhardt act at a provincial theatre. When she had told the story he took a piece of paper from the drawer of his desk and wrote on it in large block letters the name CORRIERE DELLA SERA.

'Could that have been the name of the paper that was sent to Mademoiselle Van de Velde?' he asked Madame Vize.

As the concierge read what he had written, mouthing the words letter by letter, he saw comprehension inch its way slowly into her face. 'That could have been it,' she said, astonished. 'Yes, that was the name of the paper. I am certain of it! How in the name of God did you guess?'

To show his appreciation of what she had done, Gautier escorted Madame Vize downstairs and out of the building himself. There, learning that she had come all the way from Place des Vosges by tram, he found her a fiacre to take her home, paid the driver the fare and, not wishing to offend her by offering her a *pourboire*, gave her money to buy a present for the other Sarah, her daughter's niece.

After she had left he found himself wondering how he could capitalize on the stroke of fortune which had come his way. He now knew the name of the two copies of the paper which had been sent to Ingrid and, while one could assume that they were of an article which she had written for it, he had no idea what the article was about or when it had been written and published. One way of finding out would be to contact the paper's publisher in Milan, but that would take time and he could not help feeling that time was not on his side if his coup were to succeed. Using other official channels, for example through the Italian Embassy in Paris, would also take time.

By that time it was approaching midday and Gautier decided that if he was looking for a shortcut in dealing with foreign newspapers, he could do no better than go to the Café Corneille. When he reached the café he was glad to find that most of its regular habitués were already there. As it happened luck was once again on his side and their discussion was focussed on Italy, or rather on an Italian who had announced his intention of coming to live in Paris. Gabriele d'Annunzio had achieved notoriety in his own country, partly with his licentious poems but also by his scandalous love affairs with any number of women, including the actress Eleonora Duse. Now rumour had it he was coming to live in Paris permanently with a wealthy Polish princess at her home in Avenue du Bois-de-Boulogne.

'The women of Paris are in a frenzy of sexual excitation,' the elderly judge said. 'They say that no woman can resist him.'

'And he will sleep with any woman, no matter how little physical appeal she may have,' Froissart added.

'The man is a menace to decent society. He should not be allowed to enter the country,' Duthrey said. He was in one of his most sententious moods.

'Language will be no problem. I understand he speaks ours so well that he has even written poems and a play in French.'

'And this Polish princess – does she speak Italian?' Gautier asked.

'She is learning it and she is so besotted with d'Annunzio that she has a room in her home dedicated entirely to his work and to the Italian language. Apparently she even has the Italian newspapers delivered to her every day.'

'I would not take all this very seriously, my friends,' Duthrey said. 'It is no more than rumour.'

The conversation soon drifted on to other topics, but not before Gautier had learnt enough to know exactly where on the Avenue du Bois-de-Boulogne the Polish princess had her house. Immediately after he had taken his lunch at the café in Place Dauphine he went there. When he told the manservant who opened the door who he was, he was taken without questions to the princess. She was an unusually tall woman with a mass of fair hair and a surprisingly innocent expression. In Gautier's experience very wealthy people, whatever their sex, seldom looked innocent. He told her that he was anxious to find a copy of an Italian newspaper.

'Is this part of a police investigation?' she asked.

'Not at present. It may become so.'

'And will the investigation be aimed at Commendatore d'Annunzio?'

'In no way, Princess. I have never even met the Commendatore.'

'In that case it cannot be of interest to me. I will allow you to see Aldo, my librarian. Would you mind ringing the bell for me, Inspector?'

Gautier saw a bell pull on the wall behind the Princess, pulled it and almost at once a tiny man came into the room. Gautier had heard that d'Annunzio was also very short and he wondered whether the Princess was one of those tall women who made a habit of collecting short men around them. She explained to Aldo why Gautier was there and the two of them left the room together.

The library was not large and the bookshelves which covered

its walls were not more than half-full, waiting no doubt for more works from an author who had the reputation of being prolific. A marble bust of d'Annunzio, already balding although he could not have been much more than forty when it was sculpted, was the centrepiece of the room and facing it were portraits of the poet and of Eleonora Duse on another wall. Gautier wondered at the devotion of the princess and whether there would be room for more memorabilia of d'Annunzio's mistresses, including, in due course, of herself. A table at one end of the room was covered with copies of Italian newspapers, among them several issues of the *Corriere della Sera*. Gautier told Aldo that he was looking for an article by Ingrid Van de Velde which he supposed could have been published not long before her death.

'I think I remember the article,' Aldo said and began rummaging through the collection of papers. 'It was very amusing, witty. I am sure I can find it for you.'

'Could you tell me what it was about?' Gautier asked him. 'I know no Italian.'

Aldo made a noise of disapproval. 'You should learn the language. The author poked fun at the military pretensions of Italy. As you know there is some minority support for the view that Italy should be prepared to play a major role in the European war, which everyone now believes is inevitable. As I said, the article was witty and in no way offensive. She hinted that one of the men behind the intrigues of the militarists had been a well-known Blue Beard.'

'Blue Beard?'

'Yes. Barbe-Bleu. The character in one of the stories by Perrault.' Gautier remembered reading the stories when he was a boy. Blue Beard was a man of evil reputation who had married several wives, all of whom he had killed, secreting their bodies in a hidden room.

Aldo went on, 'One other thing I recall was that the *Corriere* promised there would be a further article on the same theme the following week, but so far nothing has appeared.'

Gautier did not tell Aldo why the second article had never appeared. He was certain that it had been written, for Ingrid had always been punctilious in fulfilling her obligations and perhaps it had been in draft form among the material which Surat had found in the rubbish bin in her apartment, but if so producing it now could serve no useful purpose. As he was about to leave the Princess's home Aldo had one more piece of information to give him.

'The father of Gabriele d'Annunzio,' he said, grinning maliciously, 'used the title Commendatore, but he was never invested with the honour. His son was vain enough to do the same.'

Next morning in his office at the Sûreté Gautier thought about the note in German that Andrassy had written to Ingrid and which had been translated for him. In it Andrassy had said that he had two pieces of news: one was that Kossuth was in Paris and the other was that he had discovered the 'identity of BB'. Gautier had assumed that by BB Andrassy had been referring to the Balkan Butcher, the jocular name which he and Ingrid were thought to have given to the unknown agitator in Vienna. Now he realized that the initials could equally have stood for Barbe-Bleu. He had brought away from the library of the princess the copy of *Corriere della Sera* which Aldo had allowed him to borrow and which he would have translated as soon as possible, but in the meantime he could think of at least one more piece of stage 'business' which he should devise in readiness for his *coup de théatre*.

To do so effectively he really needed to know the protocol which would be observed at a reception sponsored by the Government similar to the one which was planned to mark the signing of the arms' contracts. Sylvie Lambert, with her knowledge of diplomatic practice, would know and he wished he had been able to ask for her advice. She had said she was going home for two days and if she had meant exactly two days she should be back in Paris in good time for the reception which the Prefect of Police had agreed to organize.

Thinking about Sylvie he realized that she was beginning to play a growing part in his work. She had helped him in London and again by introducing him to the English couple, Mr and Mrs Prynne and by giving him information about the wife of the Minister for War. Now, without thinking, he was finding a role which she might play in his coup. He could never remember any woman becoming involved in his work; his wife Suzanne certainly had taken no interest in his enforcement of the law and while Ingrid had on occasions been a useful sounding-board on political issues, she had always been too busy with her own career to wish to play any part in his. He began to wonder whether this meant that he was allowing himself to be drawn into a different kind of relationship with Sylvie and whether this was what he wanted.

Putting thoughts of Sylvie aside, he remembered that he had promised to send the Prefect of Police a list of those people who in his opinion should be invited to the reception celebrating the arms deal. Compiling it did not take long. The Minister for War was to be the host and the Prefect would know what other members of his department and government notables should be invited. Edgar Wright was at the head of the list of guests together with the 'lieutenants' who had been instrumental in helping him in his coup. Rodier was one and François Dorval was another. Although he had as yet little evidence to support his suspicions and had no idea where he could be reached, Gautier also added another name – Luca Marinetti.

*

'You have no news of my wife I suppose,' the Minister for War said.

The question and the tone of voice in which it was said showed Gautier that Gilles had not been expecting any news of his wife. There were conclusions which could be drawn from this, but Gautier was not yet ready to make them. That morning he had received from the Prefect of Police more information about the reception to celebrate the arms deal. It would be held in two days' time at the Salle Delacroix and all the people on the list which Gautier had sent the Prefect would be present. The speed with which the function had been put in place had surprised Gautier and he had decided that it would only be fair to give the Minister for War at least a hint of the role he might be called upon to play.

That was why he had called at the Minister's apartment that evening. When he had presented his personal card to the servant who answered the door, he had been admitted without question. The Minister had received him in his study and seemed friendly, even though Gautier had in effect disregarded the instructions which Courtrand and he had been given to keep the disappearance of Madame Gilles secret from everyone including their staff. He offered him a glass of port, not the fortified port which the English drank, but a rather sweet aperitif.

'I hope you will not mind, Monsieur le Ministre, if I am frank with you,' Gautier said.

'By all means.'

'Given what you have told us of the circumstances, logically there can be only two reasons for your wife's disappearance. Either she left you of her own volition—'

'She would never do that, never!'

'Or else she is being kept away from you by force.'

'But who on earth would do such a thing?'

'Could there possibly be a political reason for her abduction?'

201

Gilles hesitated, but only briefly. 'I cannot see how. I like to think that I have no political enemies.'

'Then could someone be using the abduction of your wife as a means of persuading you to take some action which you might otherwise be reluctant to follow? In America they call that blackmail I believe.'

'I would never give way to that kind of pressure.'

The total lack of conviction in Gilles's voice told Gautier that he had been right in concluding that the abduction of his wife had been used to win his approval of terms in the arms deals. Many people in the Government felt, as he did, that the deals had been too favourable to Edgar Wright's company. He also knew that he would never be able to prove it. The abduction had obviously been handled with great subtlety and even Madame Gilles might not have been aware of what was happening.

'We can only trust, Monsieur le Ministre, that she will soon be returned to you.'

That was the one slender shaft of hope which Gautier was able to hold out to the Minister for War and even as he did, he felt guilty. Now that the arms deal had been signed and would shortly be ratified, if the Minister's wife had been abducted she might well be released, but Gautier still had an uncomfortable feeling that not all would be well.

'If that happens I will always owe you a debt of gratitude, Gautier, because I am sure you will have been responsible.'

Should his coup result in the Minister and his wife being reunited Gautier would be delighted, but that was not the purpose for what he was doing. No less than four murders remained unsolved before justice could be satisfied and the rule of law in Paris restored. When he returned to his office at Sûreté headquarters he found a telegram from Sylvie waiting for him. Like all her messages it was brief and to the point: 'Will be back in Paris early tomorrow. I know you cannot wait to see me again. When and where?'

15

The Salle Delacroix was an art gallery which had paintings by Monet, Renoir and Pissarro hanging on its walls, but it had also become a fashionable venue for receptions, concerts and soirées. Gautier paid a visit there early in the day, to make sure that all the facilities he would need were available and that the police officers whom he would be bringing in could be stationed out of sight until they were required.

That morning he had sent his own *petit bleu* to Sylvie, asking her to meet him for a quick lunch at a café near Place de l'Opéra. Over the meal he had told her that the two of them had been invited to a reception that evening at the Salle Delacroix and he had only hinted at what was likely to happen. He also asked her whether it might be possible for her through her government contacts to trace the movements of foreign nationals entering and leaving France. She had told him that it was possible, but would take time as the system of checking passports was cumbersome and unreliable.

After they had finished their lunch and he was walking alone back to the Sûreté, he found himself recalling the impression which Sylvie had made on him when he had been waiting for her and she had walked into the café. In the past it had always been her personality and charm which had dominated their meetings and their conversations. That day, as he had seen her silhouetted against the entrance to the café, he had suddenly been aware of the whole woman. She was tall, he noticed and slim and her body was well-proportioned. He had never been much attracted by women whose bodies were longer than their legs, nor by those with long, rangy legs but little above to balance them. At another time thoughts like these might have led to others, but he put them aside, conscious that he had much to do before the reception that evening if his coup were to succeed.

Back in his office he sent a message to the police of the 18th arrondissement that the prisoner they were holding for the murder of the Comte d'Artagnan should be brought down to Sûreté headquarters. When Jules Magnol arrived and was brought up to Gautier's office he appeared surprisingly at ease for a man who faced the guillotine. Perhaps this meant that he was at heart a philosopher, in which case he might be more receptive to what Gautier was going to suggest to him.

Another 'ancillary' whom he needed to be present at the reception that evening was Professor Jean Cousin of the Bibliothèque Nationale. In his case it might be preferable if he arrived fairly late in the evening. One could not even be sure whether an intellectual such as he would wish to attend such a frivolous function as a reception. Gautier decided that Sylvie would be the best person to persuade him to go and to decide the timing of his arrival. Finally as Martha, the chambermaid at the Hôtel Londonderry, could not be there, Gautier arranged that both the porter and the maid from Mustapha's *hôtel de rendez-vous* should also be available when required.

After making all these arrangements Gautier called round at the Préfecture de Police. Although the Prefect had given his approval to the whole idea of a reception to celebrate the arms deal, he had since shown little interest in the arrangements for it. He must have had at least an inkling of what Gautier hoped the event would achieve, but now he was standing back from it, apparently not wishing to become involved too closely. Gautier told himself cynically that this was the typical stance of a political animal. Nevertheless he knew that the man must be told a little of what he had planned, if only so he could brief the Minister for War on how as host he should handle the reception as matters developed.

When eventually he was admitted to the Prefect's office and began outlining the arrangements he had made, the Prefect stopped him in mid-sentence. 'That is enough, Gautier! Tell me no more. I simply do not wish to know!

Early that evening Gautier arrived at the Salle Delacroix. He knew that he must be there when the reception started, but did not wish to be seen by the other guests when they arrived. An over-obvious police presence might make the guests suspicious and some of them at least might well decide not to stay for his coup to be unfurled, if that were the right word. He recalled from previous visits which he had paid to the Salle that at one end and above the main room there was a small minstrels' gallery, from which musicians could perform if music was required. There would be no music that night, but the gallery was where Gautier could conceal himself as he watched the guests arrive. That was where he went when he knew that the police officers he required to be standing by were waiting in the kitchens at the rear of the main hall.

The first people to arrive were two senior civil servants from the Ministry for War, sent presumably to check on the arrangements that had been made and the facilities available for their Minister. They walked around the premises, questioning the attendants on where the guests would be allowed to stand and from where the Minister would speak, emphasizing the protocol which must be observed. Gautier could not help being amused by their self-importance. They gave the impression that they were in charge and that the success of the reception would depend on their efficiency. Perhaps it was better they did not know that Gautier and his staff had given the Salle's attendants precise instructions on what should happen.

As the guests began to arrive, from his vantage point Gautier could see that they made up an almost random selection: politicians; more and more senior representatives of other Government departments; a small number of notable personalities from Paris society and one or two important figures from the judiciary. Gautier was pleased to see representatives from the judiciary. Although he had been fortunate enough to appear before at least two judges who were fair and reasonable, in general he felt it could do no harm for the rest of them to understand the problems which the police faced in bringing those who defied the law to justice.

The Minister for War had been advised to delay his arrival and he was not yet at the Salle when two of the men for whom the coup had been devised came into the room. Edgar Wright was accompanied by Charles Rodier and Gautier could see that they both appeared completely self-assured. Wright in particular had the air of someone who had negotiated a coup of his own and was satisfied that he had brought it to a successful conclusion. He moved through the room greeting anyone of importance whom he had met before, introducing himself to others, ready with a smile and a friendly greeting.

Another police officer was in the hall, dressed as a waiter and presently he signalled to Gautier that Magnol and the two staff from Mustapha's hotel had arrived and were waiting in the kitchens. Professor Cousin was not yet there, but Gautier was satisfied that Sylvie would bring him into the room when he was required. Timing was to be crucial to the success of what he planned and he was glad to see the Minister for War arrive. Gilles looked pale and far from happy; a sure sign, Gautier thought, that his wife had not been returned to him.

As soon as Gilles arrived, Gautier slipped down unobtrusively from the minstrels' gallery and moved in among the other guests. He saw Edgar Wright being greeted by Gilles.

'Is Madame Gilles not with you tonight, Monsieur le Ministre?' he heard Wright ask.

'No,' Gilles said lamely, 'I regret that she had another appointment.'

'Perhaps she will join you later in the evening.'

Wright's remark was what Gautier had been hoping he might hear. His plan was partly based on a hope that the reception might be used as an occasion to return Madame Gilles to her husband. The Minister for War had in effect conceded that she had been abducted and with a little ingenuity the abductor could handle her return in a diplomatic way which would avoid him facing criminal charges. If she did not appear, there were other ways in which Gautier's plan could be initiated, but the return of Madame Gilles would undoubtedly help him.

Presently some of the guests were asked to move from the centre of the hall, creating a space from where the Minister for War would make a speech welcoming the guests at the reception. One of the attendants, who was acting as major-domo for the evening, called for silence and Gilles stepped forward. He was an able speaker, articulate and fluent and after thanking the guests for coming to the reception, he expressed the Government's satisfaction at concluding an agreement which would 'help to secure the future safety of the nation' and so bring peace to France. He thanked the British firm of Lydon-Walters for the efforts it had made to meet the country's requirements and thus for their help in cementing the Entente Cordiale.

After the Minister had finished, Wright spoke. He too was a polished speaker and paid tribute to Ferdinand Gilles for 'his tireless energy and skill' which had allowed the arms deal to be concluded so swiftly. By purchasing the latest and most efficient weapons available, the Minister had guaranteed the safety of his country for the foreseeable future. Gautier supposed that he was not the only person present who saw an irony in the fact that Wright's company had concluded a similar deal, not much more than two years previously, with France's traditional enemy, Germany.

Wright had not finished speaking when the guests nearest to him stepped aside to make way for two latecomers. One of them was François Dorval and he was accompanied by a woman whom Gautier had never seen before but who, he realized at once, could only be Carlotta Gilles.

'Forgive me for interrupting you, Minister,' Dorval said loudly, 'but I met your wife at the entrance to the building and I was sure you would like her to join you.'

'Carlotta! *Chérie*!' Gilles exclaimed and then he stepped forward, took both of his wife's hands in his and kissed them. Then he added hastily, as an afterthought, 'I was so glad that you were able to come tonight after all.'

Madame Gilles was a woman of forty or thereabouts, still attractive and while her face bore none of the signs one might expect of a long captivity, she appeared confused and kept looking over her shoulder as though she were expecting someone to be following her. Her reunion with her husband had been achieved with such gallantry that everyone smiled and some could not even resist applauding. At the same time it posed a problem for Gautier. He had expected that her arrival at the reception might have given him an opportunity to intervene in Wright's speech and launch his plan. Now he would have to think of another way.

What he had not known was that the Prefect of Police had arrived unobtrusively at the Salle Delacroix and was standing at the back of those listening to Wright. Now, as Wright's speech was momentarily interrupted by Madame Gilles's arrival, he called out, 'Monsieur Wright, would you be offended if we were to ask you a question?'

'Of course not, Monsieur le Préfet,' Wright replied, 'I am delighted to see you here.'

'My question is, can we be sure that the weapons you are selling us are better than those your company has recently provided to Prussia?'

'Of course they are better.'

'Why should they be? Your sale of arms to Prussia was only concluded three years ago?'

'Monsieur, every year there are enormous advances in engineering and therefore in weaponry. The guns you have purchased from us cannot be equalled anywhere in the world.'

Gautier decided that the Prefect had given him his cue. 'And did you use the same dubious tactics to persuade the Germans to buy your arms as you have employed here in France?' he asked Wright.

'Dubious tactics, Inspector Gautier? Are you saying we used illegal methods to sell our arms to your Government?'

'We have evidence that at least four murders were committed by those whom you employed to achieve your ends.'

The astonished silence which followed Gautier's accusation was spectacular. Everyone in the hall stared at Edgar Wright, waiting for his response. His self-assurance faltered, but only for moments. Then he laughed. 'Murders? Is this some joke, Gautier?'

'I shall not catalogue the murders in the order in which they were committed,' Gautier replied. 'The last one was in some ways the most despicable. Martha was a chambermaid in a leading hotel and she was taken to a much less pretentious hotel and there brutally killed.'

'A chambermaid! You cannot be serious.'

'We have two members of the staff from the second hotel here. No doubt they will recognize the man who killed Martha, for he is in this room.'

As Gautier was speaking a policeman brought in the porter and the maid from the *hôtel de rendez-vous* who had been kept waiting in the kitchens. 'Well?' Gautier asked them.

The maid and the porter looked around the room. Dorval was standing near the front of the guests who had been listening to Wright's speech and it took them only moments to pick him out. 'That's him!' they called out. 'That's the man!'

'This is absurd!' Dorval protested. 'Why should I kill a chambermaid?'

'It was a murder to conceal another murder,' Gautier said. 'Martha saw you in the Hôtel Londonderry as you were going into the suite where the daughter of the British Ambassador was also brutally murdered.'

'Are you saying I killed Miss Macnab as well?'

'You did. Exactly why I cannot say. In revenge perhaps for ruining your life and your expectations. No doubt your reasons will become clear when you appear before an examining magistrate. In the meantime I am arresting you.'

Faced with arrest Dorval's arrogance seemed to collapse. He turned to run but by that time more police officers had come in from the kitchen and two of them grabbed him. He was led from the hall shouting and struggling. The guests who had been standing close to him backed away, some through fear, others through horror. The murder of Fiona Macnab had been widely reported in the press and had shocked Paris.

'I know nothing of these murders,' Wright said. 'You cannot implicate me or my company in them.'

'We shall see about that in due course,' Gautier said. 'Dorval was one of a group of people whom you used to help you in securing the contracts for the armaments. We have identified at least one of the others and, unless I am mistaken, here he is.'

As he was speaking Surat came into the hall, accompanied by two policemen. They were escorting Marinetti, who was smiling and did not appear disconcerted by his arrest. Surat explained that he had found him outside the hall where he had handed over Madame Gilles to Dorval who had brought her in to the reception to be returned to her husband.

'Monsieur Marinetti, you will be charged in the first instance with abducting Madame Gilles,' Gautier said.

'No, no, it isn't true!' Madame Gilles left her husband's side and went to Marinetti. 'Release him! I went with him of my own accord.'

'That may be so, but he has another charge to answer.'

'He was so good to me!' She placed her hand lovingly on Marinetti's shoulder. 'It was unbelievable! They were the best days of my life.'

Gautier glanced at her husband. The despair on Gilles's face was excruciating; all the disappointments of his married life were being relived, all the unrequited love being laid bare before him. Gautier knew there was nothing he could do to alleviate the pain. One had to be brutal.

'Marinetti,' he said, 'even if Madame Gilles does not bring charges of abduction against you, I am arresting you for the murder of a journalist with whom you shared an office in Rue Réaumur, Madame Ingrid Van de Velde.'

213

Gautier was satisfied that he had enough evidence to bring charges against Marinetti. Claude Piquet would be able to testify that he and Ingrid had dined together at his restaurant on the evening before she was murdered. Marinetti must have seen Andrassy's note to her saying he had identified *Barbe-Bleu* and as he was posing as a colleague she might even have shown it to him. Alternatively one could not rule out that he might even have had duplicate keys made to her desk. One of his reasons for taking a desk in Rue Réaumur could have been simply to spy on her. He was not to know that Andrassy had been murdered in Vienna and would never keep the appointment with Ingrid which he had suggested and at which his activities in the Balkans might have been exposed.

As part of his coup Gautier knew he must also explain the fourth of the murders which Edgar Wright and his lieutenants had contrived. He gave the policemen at the back of the hall a signal and Jules Magnol was brought forward from the kitchens where he had been kept waiting. The man did not seem unduly worried at being thrust before an audience, many of whom were distinguished figures in Paris. It was as though after his drab life in Montmartre and his arrest and interrogation for murder, he welcomed his moment of notoriety. He also knew that what he had been asked to do was his only chance of escaping the guillotine.

'Jules Magnol has confessed to the murder of Comte Eugène d'Artagnan in the Moulin de la Galette,' Gautier told his audience. 'You may be wondering at his motives and I can tell you they were simple enough. He was paid to stab the Comte to death.' He turned to Magnol. 'Now, Magnol, can you tell us if the man who paid you is here?'

Magnol looked around the room. For a long moment Gautier

thought that this theatrical gesture had failed, that Magnol would not identify the man who had paid him. Then suddenly Magnol pointed across the room.

'That's him!' he shouted. 'That's the man.'

He was pointing at Charles Rodier.

16

'Do you think that Wright and his fellow criminals will pay the price for the murders they committed?' Sylvie asked Gautier.

He understood the reasons behind her question. Much of the evidence on which his arrests had been based might at first sight seem largely circumstantial, some of it tentative, some speculative. He knew however that the processes of justice in France might be slow but they were thorough. *Juges d'instructions*, as they were called, were appointed to examine every aspect of an alleged crime. Witnesses were summoned to appear before these judges and be cross-examined, any statements which had been made would be scrutinized, checked and re-checked and every claim and counter-claim tested. Eventually a full report would be sent to a department of the Ministry of Justice known as the *Chambre de Mises en Accusations*, which would decide whether the accused would be put on trial.

In the case of the murders for which he had laid charges, *juges d'instructions* had already been appointed and had begun their work. Gautier had already made his reports to them and he was satisfied by the way their examinations were developing that Wright and his cohorts would not escape the penalty for their offences. Now for the time being he was free to travel and accept

Sylvie's invitation to visit her parents in the Dordogne. They were together in a train which, like most French trains, was winding its way deliberately, almost thoughtfully, through the countryside.

'What drove Wright to have the Comte d'Artagnan murdered?' Sylvie asked him.

'The fear of exposure. He had been one of those involved in an unpleasant homosexual scandal in Germany.'

'How could he have expected to have that kept secret?'

'The affair was hushed up because a member of the German government, a friend of the Kaiser, played a prominent part in it. Even the directors of Wright's company in England did not hear of it. If they had, he would never have been sent to France. Somehow d'Artagnan, himself a *pédé*, got to hear of it and was threatening to tell all Paris.'

'He did not give me the impression that he is homosexual,' Sylvie remarked.

'He may well not be. Wright is one of those men who is ruled by ambition. He will do anything, put on any face, make any promises to achieve his ends. And in the normal way he is clever enough to succeed without ever risking his reputation, by recruiting able and unscrupulous people to carry out his operations.'

Gautier told Sylvie that in Paris he had found Rodier, who gave him access to the wife of the Minister for War and a means of exerting pressure on him. Then there was Dorval, who had social contacts and was violent and without conscience. Finally he had Marinetti, who not only had contacts with the press, but would play a key part in Wright's next venture.

Gautier did not tell Sylvie that it was by no means certain that Wright himself would be indicted of any of the murders which his lieutenants had committed. So far no evidence had been produced linking Wright directly to the murders, although it was always possible that his lieutenants might try to exculpate their own guilt by betraying him. One murder for which Wright could not be blamed, superficially at least, was that of Ingrid. Sylvie may have guessed what was on his mind.

'Ingrid Van de Velde was a good friend of yours?' she asked him.

'One might say that.'

'If she had not died might you two have married?' Sylvie knew about Gautier's first marriage and how it had ended.

'I very much doubt it. Ingrid was too independent and too engrossed in her writing. She had been married once before and the marriage had failed, largely I believe, because she became too involved in politics. I also believe she was murdered because she was getting too close to what is happening in the Balkans.'

'What is happening?'

'The beginnings of a European war.'

Had he succeeded in arming first Germany and then France, Gautier explained, Wright's next target would have been Vienna, or perhaps Rome. When all the major European countries had spent millions on arms, war would have been inevitable.

'In some ways,' he said sadly, 'for Ingrid it was just a game, an intellectual game; exposing the men behind the intrigues. I do not believe she ever appreciated the dangers which lay ahead. Unwittingly she may have contributed to the next war.'

'But the sale of arms to France will not be ratified now, will it?'

'Wright's deal will not be, but another armaments company will soon come knocking at France's door.'

'How long do you believe it will be before the next war comes?'

'Five years, six at the most.'

Sylvie laid her hand on his arm. 'Then perhaps we should be making the most of the time that is left to us.'

Gautier smiled. 'What a good idea!' he replied.

That night Gautier lay in his bedroom recalling what had happened since Sylvie and he had left the train early in the evening. Her father had met them at the station with a pony and trap in which he had driven them the few miles to their home. Gautier had taken an instant liking to the old man and to his wife, who was waiting for them at home and who greeted him warmly, although he could not help noticing that her eyes were watchful as she looked at him.

Sylvie's father had showed him round a part of their property which was much what Gautier had supposed it would be: some arable land, but mostly orchards, enough to provide a modestly comfortable living for a family. This was the country life to which he had once been used and sharing it again brought back nostalgic memories. Over the evening meal they had drunk the local wine and afterwards he and Sylvie's father had taken a few too many glasses of an *eau-de-vie*, into the origins of which he thought it best not to enquire.

Now he lay in the darkness, looking forward to what he was sure would be a typically rural Sunday. He was on the edge of sleep when the darkness was disturbed briefly by a shaft of light and he realized that someone had come into the bedroom. It was Sylvie and she came over to his bed and lay down beside him.

'Are you sure this is wise?' he said. 'Your parents may hear.'

'Very probably they will, but it will not disturb them. We country folk do not take much account of the conventions of society.'

He could see that she was wearing only some kind of shift or chemise, so he could scarcely ask her the reason why she had come to his bed, but he knew she was a girl who would not long conceal the motives for any action she took, so he waited for her to speak.

'Jean-Paul,' she said, 'you will agree that in the past few weeks we have been getting very close. I think it is only fair that before committing yourself you should see what is on offer.'

Gautier could not stop himself laughing. 'For God's sake don't laugh!' Sylvie said. 'If my parents hear sounds of passion they will not mind, but if they hear you laughing they may conclude that you have insulted me and that will ruin the lunch they have prepared for tomorrow.'

'If you take off that ridiculous garment,' Gautier replied, 'then perhaps I can examine what is on offer.'

They both laughed. Sylvie sat up in the bed and lifted off her chemise. When he took her in his arms he could feel her trembling. He made love to her slowly and gently, caressing her breasts and stomach and thighs until he could feel her inhibitions begin to disappear. She had the body of a young girl, and like a girl she responded nervously but willingly to everything he did. When at last the climax came she could not restrain a little cry.

'That was wonderful!' She began kissing him, fierce kisses not of passion but of gratitude.

'What will your parents have thought,' he teased her, 'when they heard that cry?'

'They will have turned over in bed and gone to sleep content.' She stroked his cheek. 'You had better go to sleep as well, my love, and build up your strength for lunch tomorrow.'

Gautier knew what to expect at lunch for he had seen small tables set out at the back of the house to make a table long enough to accommodate the whole family.

'Who will be there?' he asked Sylvie.

'Everyone. My two sisters, their husbands and altogether four children of different ages, one great-grandmother at least and who knows how many cousins.'

'It sounds more like a betrothal than a family lunch.'

Sylvie's hesitation was only momentary. 'It could be,' she said.

Suddenly Gautier saw the pattern in everything that had happened since they had first met in London. Nothing had been arranged by Sylvie or by him. Their relationship had been an inevitable coming together, a natural development. He had never believed in destiny and he did not now, but if this was fate he was ready to accept it. He wanted to tell Sylvie so, but this was not the time or place. So he reached out, and drew her to him. Then he fell back on the same words he had used in the train.

'What a good idea!' was all he said.